Destiny

HUSTLER'Z LOVE 3: GAME OVER

By: Destiny T Henry

Dedication Page

To my Heavenly Father above for guiding, protecting and giving me my talents to do what I love doing.

My parents John and Persell Henry Thank you for loving me. I love y'all to pieces.

My other mother Annie Frasier. Thank you for standing beside me and helping me with everything and loving me. You have seen me turn from a 16 year old troubled teen to a grown woman with goals. Even when you saw me at my worst to now my best. Thanks mom for all your advice and love and know how much I love you.

My beautiful grandmas Christine Henry Taylor and Mary Lee Spells. I love you both my guardian angel. May you both Rest in Heaven.

My siblings: Summer Henry, Diamond Brown, Darius Brown, Destan Brown, Shavonda Dennison, Tereasa, Gavonda Heyward, Arlethia Henry, Supreme Smith, Mercedes Brown, John Smith, Jodi Brown

All my nieces and nephews.

To all my aunts and Uncles

My Godmoms: Wynnett Muhammad and Kizzie Lawson

Jeffrey Miller Jr. My lover, my friend, my everything. Baby you made me a better woman. You love me beyond all my wrong. You showed me what real love is and baby I love you beyond words.

SaQuin and Valencia Graham

Schyvaugh, Samson, Samson Jr and Amarah Lumpkin

Betty Miles: thank you for everything you have done for me and Jeff. It means a lot. Love you

Ms. Erin Ashe and Mr. Richard Berry. Thank you for all the support you continue to give me on my career and at work. Truly appreciate it.

My best friends: Myranda White, Kimberlee Morton, Paige Law, Brittany Donohue, Melissa Knox.

To my role models: Mrs. Whitney Houston (RIH), Aaliyah (RIH), Bobbi Kristina Brown (RIH), Toni Braxton, Tamar Braxton and Mr. Tyler Perry

Mrs. Gina from Kohl's. Thank you for your consist support. It means a lot to me. Thank you

To my cousin Deon Geathers and everyone who passed due to gun violence.

Granddaughter's Tears

Dedication to my Grandmother's Mary Lee Spells & Christine Henry Taylor

A granddaughter's cries when she is in your arms for the first time

When you look into her beautiful brown eyes. Your heart begins to shine.

You become her love, her strength, her everything.

Grandma, you're mine.

A Granddaughter's Tears

A granddaughter cries when you raise your voice when she wrong.

But you give her something to ease the pain

When you tell her about the birds and bees

And you make her laugh with the old school songs see.

A granddaughter's tears

A granddaughter cries when she has to say goodbye

You pass and here came all the tears I cry

I know you're in a better place.

I am going to miss your smiling face.

Watch over me my guardian angels

Until we meet again

I love you forever

guardian angels you see.

A granddaughter's tears will be.

I'll make you proud. Just wait and see.

I love you my grandmas

For eternity.

"I will not lose, for even in defeat, There's a valuable lesson learned, so it evens up for me."-Jay Z

Recap from Last Chapter of HL2

SNAKE

I read a quote that said:

"The only thing I regret about my life is the length of it. If I had to live my life again, I'd make all the same mistakes - only sooner." (Tallulah Bankhead)

Now that the shit was going down with my wifey, it was time to get rid of that nigga Roc. I went with Red as she met up with her crew.

Tonight got to be the night to do this shit. We have to end this nigga once and for all.

Maybe that was a sign to get the fuck out of the game. It was time to give that shit up and live a normal life.

I grabbed Red's arm before we headed into the warehouse.

"Red, look I love you. The worst thing that I did was leave you and our daughter. I never knew how much you meant to me until I almost lost you. I don't want to feel like that ever again. Let's get away. Let's quit this shit once and for all. We can go and get married and start a family just like we always wanted to." I suggested as someone walked up clapping their hands.

I turned around looking at Harlem as she strolled up. Her eyes were blood shot red as if she had been crying all day. The look on her face told me that it wasn't a social call. It was more like a 'get even' call.

"Bitch, are you happy. I told you to stay the fuck away from my daughter and you couldn't! You had to go up there huh? Well I guess now you got what you wanted! Aniya is dead and so are you." Harlem spat.

She drew her gun without hesitating and released a single shot towards Red. She fell to the ground instantly. Without thinking, I pulled out my piece delivering one deadly round into her chest. I watched that crazy bitch gasp for air. That's when I put one between her eyes...

I turned around looking at Red lying on the ground. *"This shit can't be happening,"* I cried kneeling down beside Red's body.

"Red, come on baby get up. Help me! Someone help me!" I yelled pulling Red up in my arms as the crew ran up out of nowhere.

"Yo, what the fuck happened to Queenie. Yo, we need to get her to the hospital. Snake we need to go now. "HB pleaded.

I quickly picked Red up and we ran to the car.

"Lord, please don't let her die."

Arriving at the hospital within minutes, I held Red rocking her lifeless body. Just the thought of losing her had my mind in a very dark place.

Not being able to resist, I laid on her on the stretcher and watched it roll off. That's when my heart hit the floor along with my body.

I lost my mother, my daughter, and now just the thought of losing Red.... I didn't know what the fuck I was going to do.

Toni ran up in the hospital. Her eyes were swollen and puffy. She walked up to me slapping me across the face. I accepted it and pushed past her. I had to get out of there. H.B. stopped me as I passed the waiting room.

I started pacing back and forth as he placed his hands on my shoulder.

"Yo, Snake, I think it's time that we handle this situation. It needs to end." H.B. whispered as if he had some information.

"You right nigga. Get Ace and DMack. Tell them that we need to go on a little field trip. It's time to handle this nigga once and for all." I replied as Toni grabbed my arm and dragged me outside of the waiting area.

"Reggie I know right now everything seems to be going wrong and it is, but this won't solve anything. If you love my daughter like you say you do, you wouldn't do this. It's a bad idea Reggie. Nothing good is going to come out of what you are about to do. Please think about Kera. Think about what she would want you to do, and I know this ain't it. Please." She begged.

Fuck what she was talking about. It was one thing for that punk ass nigga to come at me, but when he came after my family it was time for war. I knew exactly where he was going to be.

Roc owned a little piece of shit night club on East 96th street, that he called 'Pussy Popping Bitches.' Well I guess you could understand why he named it that. It wasn't like he had bad ass bitches up in there popping ass.

After a few minutes, we pulled up to this cheap ass crappy building. It was a shithole for real.

I stepped out the car making sure that my gun was loaded. I knew how that nigga was. He had niggas all over that raggedy ass building.

"Nigga you must be lost or something to be rolling your ass up in here son. I thought that it was a lie that you was back in town. Yo, nigga let me offer up my condolences. I heard that Red was shot. Sorry to hear that bro. What the fuck do you want nigga? It better be a good reason why your ass walked up in my shit." Roc threatened causing me to pull out my piece and aim it at his head.

"Son, give me one good reason why I shouldn't splatter your brains all over this motherfucking place right now." I warned as he stood up with his boys standing right behind me.

They drew down, but didn't do shit. That didn't scare me. That day I came prepared to die for mine.

"Snake, nigga you don't want to come at me with that shit alright. Nigga you ain't nothing but a little bitch. Be a man and pull that trigger.... I thought not. Nigga get your bitch ass up out of my spot before I bust a cap in your ass." He laughed while giving me a view of his back.

"Who the fuck does this motherfucka think that he is turning his back to me?"

"Yo, Roc..." I started shifting my body in his direction.

Soon as our eyes met, I pulled the trigger. The bullet entered the front of his forehead and came out of the back, sending brain matter all over the room.

"Oh shit!" One of Roc's boys shouted as they all stood at attention. They had no choice but to react once H.B. and Ace pulled out their pieces and started blasting off.

Gun shots and screams sounded off throughout the building as the girls took off running to the nearest exit. I tapped my niggas as we took off out the door jumping into the car. I thought I would be happy finally taking Roc's ass out, but all I could do was think about Red.

After all the shit that Roc had done to my wifey, to Sophia, and to me, the nigga was lucky that all that he got was a bullet to the head. I could have and should have done a hell of a lot worst.

I was totally disgusted by everything that was going on. I needed to sit my ass down somewhere. Soon as I popped a squat, my phone rang and sent my heart straight to my feet.

"Hello, yes, what? I am coming now. I will be right there." I replied as I received info that Red had taken a turn for the worst.

"Snake, what's up?" H.B. questioned once he saw that I couldn't get the words couldn't come out, but he knew.

"We gotta go!"

We hopped in the car and H.B. hit the gas speeding up to get me to the hospital.

"What the fuck am I going to do now?" I thought the whole way there. "Please let her pull through."

We finally made it to the hospital. It seemed to take forever and a damn day.

Before H.B. could stop, I jumped out the car running into the hospital. The words played through my head as I made my way to the waiting room where Toni was.

I walked in finding Toni sitting in the chair close to the window. Her head was clutched in her hands with tears rolling down her fingers.

"This can't be happening right now."

"Where is she? I need to see her." I pleaded as Toni lifted her head.

She didn't say a word. She rose to her feet taking my hand to lead me where Red was.

"She is so strong. She is a fighter. There is no way in hell that she is gone. She can't be!" I thought trying to convince myself that this was just a lie.

Toni stopped in front of the door where Red was laying on the table inside. She allowed me to go in by myself.

Tears cascaded down my face as I gazed upon the woman I loved laying there hooked up to all the machines. They were the only reason she was breathing. Without them she was gone. We had to make a decision. I knew that I couldn't do it, so I left it up to Toni.

I couldn't help but to gaze upon my woman one last time while she was still alive. She was so damn beautiful, even in the state she was in. Bending down, I kissed her lips thinking that she would open her eyes, but she didn't.

"How am I supposed to live life without her?"

I couldn't take it. I stepped out and told Toni how I felt. She understood and agreed.

HB walked up moments later. His face was turned up and I could see his frustration. Before I had a chance to question him, he hauled off and punched a hole into the wall. I put my ill feelings aside and grabbed a hold of my partner helping him up. I didn't know if any of us would ever be the same again.

****

It had been a couple of hours since I left the hospital and my whole world had completely hit rock bottom. H.B. had been calling me, but I didn't feel up to talking to anyone. I had to deal with living my life without Red. No one could begin to imagine what hell I was feeling.

After losing my mother I never thought that my life would be the same again. Yet, it was because I encountered Red.

For the first time in my life I met a woman that could touch my heart. Even though I hurt her and caused her so much pain. I loved her in my own way. Then I lost my bro Ty and that shit almost destroyed a nigga. When my mother died that nigga was the one that held me down allowing me to come and live with him. Man that shit tore me up.

I tried pulling myself together enough to handle the loss of my little girl. I still didn't know how to do that...

Now losing Red was about to be a loss on a whole other level. I tell you one thing; I knew that I would never be the same. I realized that we had our problems in the past but she was my right hand. She was my everything...

After a while, Toni came through. I couldn't even face her. She tried to talk to me but I wasn't ready.

"Reggie, I need to talk to you," she urged as if it was a damn emergency. I didn't want to hear shit about how Red stopped breathing as soon as they pulled the plug. I didn't want to envision that shit.

"My life is so incomplete." I thought silently as I closed myself in Red's room locking myself inside.

I grabbed my gun as it lay beside the forty that I had been drinking on. It was the second one in two hours.

"I won't live my life without her." I thought as I loaded the gun with one bullet.

"There's something you need to know!" Toni shouted through the door.

"I am so sorry Toni." I whispered. "I don't want to hear it."

Before I changed my mind, I pulled the trigger.

BANG!!!!!!!!!!!!!!!!!!

Well Damn....

Chapter One

ACE

A wise person once stated: "The worst kind of pain is when you're smiling. Just to stop the tears from falling." (Unknown Author)

I pulled up to Toni's house to check on my big brother as I heard the shot. Before I could think twice, I jumped out the car and ran into the house. I could hear Toni as she screamed out Snake's name while banging on the door, but Snake wouldn't respond.

Running up the stairs my heart began to pound rapidly. Maybe it was the fear of knowing that my brother had done something stupid.

The emotions continued running through my head as I hoped and prayed that Snake didn't off himself. Shit, was really fucked up in the game right then.

The news of Queenie's current condition spread through the streets like a wild fire that you couldn't put out. On the real, I couldn't even begin to imagine what the fuck my bro could possibly be going through. Nigga if that shit was me I would have thought about offing myself too. Shit, the game was hard without a loyal shorty.

Man, he loved Queenie. I knew he did even when he didn't show it. Now she was in a coma fighting for her life. I am telling you man. That shit was really fucked up.

Finally, hitting the top step, Toni continued to pound on the door. Still there was no response.

"I got it." I said catching my breath before using my side to bust into the room. I came to a quick stop ass I looked down at Snake laying in a pool of blood.

"Hell no nigga, you can't go out like this!" I thought to myself as I kneeled down beside my brother.

"Toni! Call 9-1-1. Yo, hold on Bro! I need you to hold on!" I said repeatedly.

Blood continued to drip out from the wound in his head. What the fuck man? I reached in; checking to see if he was gone. Suddenly Snake grabbed ahold of my hand. Tears rolled down his cheek.

Maybe he became emotional due to his unsuccessful attempt at killing himself. Damn, I had never seen that nigga cry before then. The shit was really serious man.

"Nigga, I need you to hang in there. Don't you die on me you son of a bitch? Come on man keep your eyes open motherfucker." I pleaded as he began mumbling something over and over again. In my mind I was thinking more about what was going on with my brother. I moved in closer trying to hear what he had to say.

"Let me die! I just want to die! I need to die!" he whispered repeatedly as he began drifting in and out of consciousness.

"Where in the hell is that ambulance? Snake, hang in there please!" I begged. Looking at my brother like that made me sick to my motherfucking stomach.

The ambulance finally pulled up as I continued holding onto my brother's hand. I began wondering what the hell was going to happen right then. I began questioning.

"How the hell did we get here? How the hell could someone lose everything and everyone plus lose himself in the mix?"

I kept asking myself but the shit just didn't make any fucking sense. I didn't know where to begin to find the motherfucking answer either.

I sat in the waiting room pacing back and forth while waiting on the doctor to come out and let a nigga know what the fuck was going on with my brother. I could hear that bitch ass nigga HB talking to the nurse at the nursing station about Snake. To be honest I didn't even know why that motherfucker was even there. Nigga sat there acting as if he truly gave a damn about my brother and what the fuck he was going through right then. When he didn't...

My face was sour as that fake ass nigga walked in with the local thot Sophia on his arm. Those two shouldn't have even been there; on the real.

"What's good Ace? What the fuck happened Kid? Niggas on the block said Snake shot himself. Yo, what happened? Talk to me son." He said as I tried to keep my cool. That nigga needs to get out of here with all that fake ass shit. Nigga had me fucked up.

"First, of all nigga I'm not your son. Let me make it clear to you about another thing HB. You may have fooled Snake and Queenie with your bullshit but I ain't them. I can see past it. I don't fuck with little bitch ass niggas like you." I said pushing past him heading out the door.

Outside I pulled out the half of joint that I was trying to save for my bro. Shit, with everything that was going on, I needed it more than ever.

I tried to clear my head from all the shit that was going on. I mean first losing my grandma due to a drive by shooting of some little punk ass niggas. I was still waiting to find them fools. Then, Queenie got shot by that bitch Harlem who was supposed to be her mother.

It was hard as hell seeing, sitting, and visiting Queenie every day while she was on life support until the day the doctor told Toni that she would not recover and she had to pull the plug and now my brother shooting himself. The shit had a niggas mind all over the place. Damn, what the hell else could possibly go wrong?

"Ace?" Miguel called out.

Damn, I guess I was wrong.

"Yo, what the fuck are you doing here nigga? Ain't no one invited you here kid? You better get the fuck out of here son." I warned lifting my shirt flashing my 9mm.

"Put your shirt down nigga. We come here in peace." Miguel assured.

"Who the fuck is we son?" I asked as my pops walked up.

Yo, this nigga can't be serious right now.

He was rolling with the enemy. Didn't he know that the nigga rolled with Roc? You know the same nigga that called himself trying to take out my brother. We were beefing with that nigga. What the fuck was my pops doing with him? What now that the nigga didn't have Roc he wanted to come to our crew? Hell no. I didn't trust that nigga and nothing was going to change that.

"Yo, pops what's up with this? Why the fuck is this nigga here?" I said getting even more pissed off. That nigga couldn't be serious.

"Ace, look ain't nobody here for no drama or nothing. Word is that Snake ain't doing too well. Nigga what happened?" Black asked as I exhaled still looking at that nigga. Nigga wanted to act as if he gave a damn, when he never really fucking did.

"Look, Snake's still in surgery, but to be honest the shit don't look to good. Come on man." I said taking one last puff before flicking my roach.

I couldn't stand the idea that my pops was rolling with that motherfucker. Shit, if Snake wasn't in this situation Miguel would have gotten fucked up. Snake never trusted that nigga and neither did I.

I walked back into the waiting room as Black and Miguel walked in behind. DMack, Big 9, and that nigga HB rose to their feet.

"Yo, Ace what the hell is this nigga? You want to bring this little bitch here? Now kid really. Where your brother is fighting for his life. K.I.D.?" HB clowned.

"You want to repeat that nigga, huh? Cause I've been waiting a little minute to knock your bitch ass out." Miguel warned as HB made his way over to him. That was when my pops intervened.

"You niggas better get it together. I invited Miguel. You all better remember what the hell I taught y'all. Bro's before anything else. Now look, one of your bro's is in there fighting for his life and y'all want to be out her battling over a fucking area. Y'all better get your shit together." Black advised as Miguel walked over to a corner.

What the hell did my father mean by bro's before anything else? That nigga wasn't my bro. *Fuck outta here.*

The only ones I even considered my brothers were ZMoney and Trigga. I had been rolling with those dudes for a minute.

Those niggas already knew what it meant when my pops broke shit up. He was an old school nigga. They only talked once and didn't you dare swing back. That nigga didn't have a problem laying you out right in a hospital.

I witnessed my pops slagging a nigga down for swinging on him when he tried to resolve a problem. Shit, imagine what he would do to those niggas.

Hours past and still no clue to what the hell was going on back there. I looked at the door as my new shorty Monica walked in looking good as fuck. Baby girl was everything that I ever wanted. Shit, after being with that crazy bitch Paula who also fucked my pops and got pregnant by him I was cool on her. Monica was my world now. I never met someone who could make me feel the way that she did.

The doctor walked in and I could feel my heart drop to the floor. My wifey grabbed a hold of my hand as it began to shake.

"The bullet pierced the cerebral cortex which is the outer layer of the brain. I am sorry there's nothing that we can do." The doctor stated hesitantly. He seemed to be beating around the bush.

"Doc, what the hell are you telling us? Is my brother dead?" I inquired as Monica rubbed my hand.

"Right now he is breathing with the assistance of a ventilator. He is in a coma. I'm sorry. Right now it is just a waiting game to see if he is going to ever wake up." The doctor answered honestly.

After hearing that fucked up news, I became even more pissed off. Soon as the doctor walked away, I punched a hole into the wall.

Monica grabbed a hold of me. I tried to fight back my tears but that shit hurt like hell man. To know that my brother was laying in a coma not knowing rather or not he was going to make it. I swear that shit was tearing me up inside man.

I walked into the room looking at Snake. My nigga was just lying there not moving. He appeared helpless.

Everyone was holding out for hope but to be honest I thought that he was gone already. It was like the machine was doing all the breathing for him but he wasn't really there.

It had been a couple of days since that shit happened. My pops hadn't left Snake's bedside. No one knew what to think at that moment.

There was one thing that I did know though. Snake didn't need no fake ass two timing ass nigga around him. I knew that for a fact.

When I walked into the room, my heart continued to cry. It hurt so much to see my brother in pain like that. It reminded me all over when my grandmother who was more like a mother to me died.

I never knew my mother but my 'G-Mom' was my everything and now seeing Reggie that way man. I didn't know what the fuck to do.

I leaned in to whisper in my brother's ear. My words were for him only.

"I got you bro. Ain't no one safe. They will all pay for this nigga. Don't you worry." I promised kissing my brother on the head as Monica walked up.

"You ready babe?" She asked grabbing ahold of my hand.

My pops made it to where he was the only one allowed to stay at Reggie's bedside. I guess he wanted to be a security guard as well as his pops.

All those years and that nigga never did right by his kids. I had to give it to him though. He was trying to make shit right with Reggie. Shit that was the least he could do.

We never knew when Reggie's heart was going to stop beating. That was, if it hadn't already.

Chapter Two

HB

A wise person once said: "All bullshit aside now it's time to be honest, I fear no man for death is all that's promised." (50 Cent)

Those streets needed a new King of East Harlem now that the bitch ass nigga Snake was now in a coma. Sorry ass son of a bitch couldn't even off his self correctly.

I couldn't lie and say that he didn't have it coming because he did. Red's death, my bro Ty's death, shit even his own mother's death was all his motherfucking fault. Nigga thought that the whole world was supposed to bow down and kiss his ass like some little bitch. *Humph, look who the bitch is now*.

Shit, I didn't even know how I could have even stayed friends with someone like him. Nigga used to think he was the shit because of who his father was. That nigga Black ain't been shit for a long time and truth if you ask me he still wasn't shit.

I walked up to Snake's hospital room as Black stood guard.

"What the fuck this nigga a fuck security guard or something." I thought to myself.

"HB, what the fuck are you doing here nigga? I guess you ain't got my memo yesterday. No one wants you here. Be out cuz." Ace spat walking up behind me.

Yo, on the real I was seriously starting not to like that little motherfucker. That nigga really didn't want it with me.

"Look you little dumb motherfucka. I stayed off your ass out of respect for your pops and Snakes. Get it trusted, I ain't the one to be disrespected. I blast motherfuckers for running their mouths. Trust if you keep trying my nigga you will be next." I warned.

I swear I was about two seconds off of his little ass. That fool had better count his lucky stars. Cause man if he kept fucking with me he would be lying flat on a stretcher right next to his bitch ass brother.

"Nigga, you don't put no fear here cuz. Stop sitting here acting like you give a fuck about my brother. You a fake ass nigga that was waiting for my brother to get killed or die so that you could take control of the crew and the streets. I know little bitch ass niggas like you. You want to act like you're a true friend when all you're looking for is an opportunity. Yeah nigga I know all about you and trust your day is coming. I am gonna let you live right now, but let me make this clear to your little pathetic ass. Stay the fuck away from my brother cuz before I show you what this little nigga can do." He spat before walking into the room closing the door behind him.

I stood looking in the doorway as that little nigga dapped up his pops. I'm telling you that the little nigga had no idea what the hell he was getting himself into coming for me. I guaranteed if he kept it up his ass will end up like his bitch ass brother and I wasn't playing either.

Strolling through the block, I thought about my next move while watching everyone sitting around whispering and crying over that lame ass nigga Snake. *Man, fuck that nigga man.*

I wanted to be the man making all the loot. Those niggas out there weren't going to wait for no fix and neither was I. As far as I was concerned that nigga Snake was already dead.

I turned the corner only to spot Sophia sitting on the steps next to Rico's convenience store. She was waiting on me.

"Damn, baby girl is looking just right in that hot pink jumper squeezing her body in all the right places."

It was showing off all her sexy curves. With it she wore a hot pair of six inch platform back lace side zip black ankle boots. I swear that girl knew just how to make a nigga hard. Just looking at her made my dick stand up at attention.

I'm telling you baby girl made me yearn for her touch.

"Hey babe. You alright?" she asked.

Sophia leaned in as her lips met mine. The warmness of her lips sent chills down my spine. She threw her arms around my neck as I lost myself in her fruity kiss. I could still taste the traces of the Bud light Lime Straw-Berry Rita Malt as it lingered on her tongue.

"Hell no everything aint alright! These niggas man. I swear it seems like Snake got them brain washed or something. Babe, they are sitting at the hospital like some little bitches instead of going out there and getting back to work. I mean what the fuck? Niggas forgetting that we need to eat. I mean damn, the shit that's happening to him. He did that shit to his motherfucking self and I don't feel bad about the condition that his in. You know." I admitted as she passed me a forty.

"Listen babe, I was actually thinking about that. Why don't you start your own crew? I mean there's absolutely no one to stop you. You can bring on DMack, Big 9, Z Money, and Trigga." Sophia suggested as if she had the shit all planned out.

"What if they don't want to? What if they want to be loyal to that nigga Snake? Then what?" I asked taking a sip.

"Then we will kill there ass. It's our turn babe. With Roc gone, Red gone and Snake almost

out the door, there's no threat. We can rule all of
Harlem. Plus, my cousins True and Real said that
they would be down with you." Sophia added.

Damn, see this was why I loved that bitch
man. Baby girl always had shit on point for your
boy. Man, and for her to get True and Real to join
with me said a whole fucking lot.

Those niggas were the realest, cruelest sons
of bitches that I ever dealt with. I met them one
summer when I went up to Bed-Stuy to meet
Sophia's old man for the first time. Those niggas
were there grilling a motherfucker down.

They took me to their spot and I witness
first hand as True cut off a crackheads arm for
stealing his shit and lying to him. Meanwhile, Real
placed a bullet right in between the crack heads
eyes. To be honest the person was so fucked up
you couldn't tell if it was a he or she. I mean those
nigga put in work on that piece of shit. Hopefully
when the time came they will do a number on that
big mouth little nigga Ace.

"On the real ma, i hope these niggas don't
turn shit up on me and not want to be down with
your boy cause then their ass will end up like
Snake. Shit, I would hate to do that to my bros but

fuck it. Money before anything else. That brother code died along time ago. After my bro Ty was killed. You know now it was every nigga for himself." I explained.

"How about you handle your business and I'll be waiting back at home for you in your favorite outfit... Umm you know. Don't keep me waiting all night HB. "She warned kissing me yet again before walking off twisting her ass as she did so.

Damn, baby girl is going to get it when I get home.

Deciding to take shorty's advice, I met up with those nigga to see where their heads are at. Hopefully the fools chose to roll with me cause I would hate to kill one of my own boys.

Sometimes, that was the motherfucking sacrifice you had to make when you were trying to take over I guess. I would just have to see how shit turned out. Time would definitely tell.

****

Me and the boys met up on our old stomping grounds. I could tell from the hurt on their faces that they were going through it over that clown ass nigga Snake. I didn't know what for. That nigga don't give a fuck about no one but himself.

"Yo. What's good my nigga? What did you call us here for. Furthermore, why ain't Ace here?" BIG9 inquired.

Damn, this nigga don't waste any time.

Well shit let's get down to it then.

"I didn't invite that nigga. He is sitting at his brother bedside, but listen niggas, I didn't come here to talk about that nigga Snake alright. I am here to talk business. We need to get back to these streets and make some money. Under a new niggas command. I think that nigga should be me." I stated confidently hoping that everyone would agree.

"Yo, nigga are you motherfucking serious right now? My bro is laying up in the motherfucking hospital fighting for his life, while your bitch ass is sitting talking about some take over the game bullshit? Now I see why you didn't want Ace here. You sneaky motherfucker. Fuck outta here. Nigga, now I see what Black used to tell us to watch out for niggas that's trying to come over in the midst of a tragedy cause those niggas motives are dangerous. What's your motives nigga, huh?" BIG9 questioned curiously.

I knew that the motherfucker would be a problem. Nigga listened to all of Snakes bullshit. Nigga though that he was a saint. Fuck out here with that shit.

"Man, Snake's a bitch! Y'all think that nigga gives a damn about you. He don't. That nigga didn't even give a fuck about Queenie. Shit, look what happened to her man. Come on son. Shit is fucked up right now. My pockets are hurting niggas and I know yours are too. I got a little shorty to take care of man." I explained as BIG9 clapped his hands.

I could see right then that the motherfucker was going to be a problem. Dead ass.

"Nigga shut the fuck up. You will never be Snake nigga no matter what you try to do. I'm out." BIG9 huffed as I pulled out my 9mm and pointed at that niggas head as soon as he turned around.

"Nigga, please don't make me do this." I replied nodding my head.

"Nigga, you pull a gun on me. Nigga have you lost your motherfucking mind? Pull the trigga nigga. No matter what you do I ain't joining your ass. I am loyal to my nigga Snake son on the real." He huffed.

"Fine." I smirked pulling the trigger.

I watched as that nigga fell to the ground face first. Shit, I knew that it was against the rules to shoot a motherfucker from behind but the nigga fucking disrespected me.

Don't you ever turn your back to me and then talk shit. Fuck outta here with that fake shit.

"Nigga you are on some straight bullshit! That shit wasn't fucking necessary." DMack spat. Now that nigga wanted some of me.

"Anyone else?" I threatened. "Now this is how the shit going to go. Either you join me or you join this nigga right here. Make your choice now."

I stood there and I waited. Those niggas knew better than make me wait longer than I motherfucking had to or there would be another dead body to join the one already on the floor.

"You are one crazy motherfucker but we are down." DMack acknowledged as the other two motherfuckers shook their head.

"Good now Trigga you and that nigga ZMoney get rid of this motherfuckers body. Better yet throw this fat sloppy ass piece of shit in the ocean and let the shark chew his ass the fuck up. DMack arrange a meeting with that nigga Kevin. It's time to take over."

Niggas wasn't moving fast enough for my taste. I had to yell some more to make those motherfuckers start moving.

"What the fuck are y'all waiting for?" I questioned as I watched them leave.

When they were gone, I pulled out my cell phone texting True and Real. I had to meet up with those niggas then introduce them to the rest of our team.

Chapter Three

Ace

It had been a couple of days and shit still wasn't looking too good for Snake nor Red. Man, I tell you what, the shit had a niggas head fucked all the way up.

I continued to ask myself how the fuck did we end up there. The more I thought about it the madder I got.

I wiped away the tears that fell from my eyes as I approached Queenie's room. They said that real men ain't supposed to cry but that was some bullshit. Real men wasn't dealing with the shit that I was forced to face.

Looking at two people you love fight for their lives was some heavy shit. To make things worse, we still didn't know if they were going to make it.

When I entered Red's room, I saw Toni seated in the chair beside Red's bed. She was gripping onto her hand as tears continued to pour down her face.

Damn, man seeing Queenie like that was fucked up. You never truly knew how much someone meant to you until you were looking at them with tubes down their throat helping them to breathe.

I couldn't begin to imagine the pain that Toni could be going through but shit, she did it to herself. Who was I to judge though? Shit I wasn't always there for my brother either.

Sometimes I felt like I didn't do my best by Snake. Sometimes it felt like it was all my fault.

"Hey Toni, how is Red doing?" I inquired as she wiped her eyes looking up at me. The expression on her face said it all.

"The same. The doctors came in today and said they though it was a slim chance that she is going to recover from this. I keep praying that God brings my baby through this. I can't lose her Ace. I... I can't." She cried.

The tears that once dried up began pouring down yet again. I placed my palms on her shoulder as she grabbed ahold of my wrists.

"Queenie is a fighter Toni. You know like I know she is going to fight until she can't fight anymore. Just like my brother. They will be alright." I said hoping for the best but also trying to prepare myself for the worst.

"Code Blue ICU Room 315! Code Blue ICU Room 315!" The nurse yelled over the intercom.

"What the fuck that's Snakes room?" I questioned myself as I looked at Toni.

She shook her head as I ran out the room. My heart pounded rapidly though my chest. Everything, nothing, just anything went through my head.

As I approached the room, my father sat on the cold floor with his hands clutching his head. My stomach hit my feet as the doctors walked out. Their heads hung low.

This shit can't be happening again.

"I'm sorry to tell you this but Reggie's heart stopped again. We tried bringing him back but we couldn't. I'm sorry." The doctor informed regretfully.

The tears couldn't stop pouring down my face if I wanted them to. I eased past the doctor walking in the room. Reggie was lying on the bed with his eyes closed as if he was sleeping. He looked at peace finally. No more trying to live a life that wasn't fit for him. Damn, sometimes I wanted to blame my pops. That shit was all his fault. If he wasn't trying to make us like him my Brother would still be here.

"Don't you worry big bro. I am going to make sure all these motherfuckers pay for this. Trust and believe that." I said kissing him on the head before leaving the room. Now that my brother was gone for real, I didn't know what the fuck I was going to do.

"Ace!" My father shouted as I continued walked past him. I didn't want to hear a motherfucking thing he had to say. He killed my brother.

Well he might as well have. He introduced him to this fucking lifestyle and now look where it got him, dead.

As I was in the hallway, bitch ass HB walked up beside me while I waited on the elevator. The last thing I wanted to do was listen to anything that sorry ass motherfucker had to say. Today would be the day that I put that motherfucker in the morgue. *Let him try me.*

"My condolences Ace. If you need me let me know." He said with a fake ass smile on his face.

I didn't trust that fool. He was fake as fuck and I didn't roll with folks like that.

"Fuck you nigga. I don't give a fuck about your condolences. Stay away from me and mine including my sister in law. Don't try me motherfucker cause if you know what's best for your sorry ass you'll stay far the fuck away from Red. Forewarning..." I spat as the elevator doors opened.

I entered then turned around and faced that fool. He was just standing there with a dumb as smirk. Stupid ass motherfucker...

I grabbed my phone to dial Big 9. I hadn't heard from that nigga all motherfucking day. It wasn't like him. He would've have been there.

No answer. Fuck. Let me dial up DMack.

"What's up Ace? Snake alright?" He asked as I stood there in dead silence.

"Ace, what the fuck is going on? My nigga, you aint sayin' shit. Yo, is Snake good?" DMack asked again.

"Snake died about 15 minutes ago DMack. Look, I need you and Big 9 to meet me. We need to talk about some shit." I informed him before I headed off to the elevator.

As a body was rushed passed me, I wondered who the fuck it could be. I thought to myself.

"Yo, nigga Big 9 is missing." He revealed.

"What the fuck you mean Big 9 is missing? Nigga meet me in fucking 10." I instructed before hitting the 'end' button.

There was no way that Big 9 could be missing. Something shiesty had to be going on.

I waited patiently. It fucking seemed like forever for DMack to arrive.

"Damn, about time!" I thought to myself as he finally turned the corner.

Eyeing him carefully, I noticed that something seemed to be off about that motherfucker. I couldn't tell if it was just me or my perception of shit right then.

Right now I don't trust anybody. Especially niggas that are gonna try to benefit off of Snake's death.

"Yo, bro how are you holding up? I know how you feel about your brother and shit. But trust that nigga Snake will never be forgotten. You know what I'm saying?" DMack assured.

As I looked at that nigga, I wondered when the fuck he started caring about my brother. The only nigga that was truly down for my brother was gone and the other one was missing.

"Whatever nigga. Look when is the last time that you talked to that nigga Big 9? I mean shit. No one has heard nothing from that nigga. This shit ain't like him. Look I am going to ask around and see if anyone heard anything." I informed DMack.

He just stood looking puzzled and shit. *Man, what the fuck is wrong with this nigga man?*

It was a second or two before that fool snapped out of it. I didn't know what was up with that shit.

"No doubt nigga. I will hit you up if I hear anything." DMack promised.

I dapped that nigga up still thinking that something wasn't fucking right. Big 9 would never just fucking leave without say a word to anyone. Hell no. He would never leave my brothers side.

"Trust, I'm gonna find out what the hell is going on around this motherfucker. Somebody is gonna tell me something!"

I stomped through the streets asking every motherfucker I came across if they had seen my nigga Big 9. Everyone wanted to play dumb and shit but I knew somebody knew something.

Putting my street rampage on pause, I started heading back to the crib. I had one stop to make on the way.

I had to meet up with the connect to get me a dime bag or something. The shit a nigga was going was stressful like a motherfucker.

What I really needed was to smoke me a dozen of L's. That shit right there would have my ass in a nice daze for real.

After turning up the block, I rolled up to the spot. When I did, that nigga Kevin stood outside his apartment. It seemed like he was waiting on someone. I hadn't talked to the fool so I know it wasn't me he was expecting.

"Yo, Kevin what's up nigga?" I greeted with a head nod.

"What's good kid? How's Queenie doing? Oh yeah, and my condolences about your bro. Shit, is fucked up right now through."

"Why you say that Kev?"

"Word is that HB is trying to take over Snake and Red's old spot. They said two new niggas from Bed-Stuy is here and have joined forces with that nigga. Watch you back Ace. Now that Snake is gone you're a threat." Kevin revealed knowing that I didn't give a fuck about those niggas.

"Nigga you worry to fucking much. Look Queenie is fine and shit. I aint worried about HB or his pussy ass crew. Talking about that shit, have you heard from Big 9?"

"Na nigga I haven't. I have been calling him for 3 days now but I aint got no answer."

"Aight then, oh yeah, I need a dime bag." I requested reaching for my wallet.

"Look, this one is one me. Be careful young blood. There's a bullet out there that they say has your name on it." He warned and nodded.

"Don't worry about me. I'm good my nigga. I'll get with you later." I shrugged before heading in the opposite direction.

I ain't worry about two niggas from Bed-Stuy. If they know what's good for them they would be worried about me.

I entered the house and peeped Monika standing in the kitchen. The aroma from the baked chicken, baked Mac and cheese and my favorite collard greens lingered throughout the house.

Stepping into the kitchen, I crept up behind Monika and kissed her neck. She quickly turned around.

By the way she stared at me I knew word had got back to her about Snake. When she followed up by throwing her arms around me, it was confirmed. *Damn, this feels so good.*

"Baby, are you okay? Your father came through and told me that Snake died. He was also looking for you." Monika explained.

"Man, fuck that nigga. Alright? I don't want him to step foot back in my crib." I snapped.

Suddenly, out of the blue I heard his voice. I caught me off guard and I didn't like the shit one damn bit.

"We need to talk kid" Black said as I turned around.

What the fuck is this? Is this nigga in my crib alone with my lady? Hell no, I ain't going for this shit again.

The last time I left that clown in my house with one of my chicks he fucked them. That shit wasn't happening again. I loved Monika way too much for that shit. *This girl is my world man.*

Being with Monika had made me want to be a better man. Plus, the shit that she had been through made me never want to hurt her; never.

"Right now I ain't got shit to say to you. I don't ever want you in my crib if I ain't here. You got that." I threatened as I continued to the table and took out my bag of weed.

"I'm gonna let you slide on how the fuck you're talking to me because you're grieving and shit, but there will never be another time where you think you can talk to me like that. You got me little nigga?" he checked as I rose to my feet to look him in the face.

"Yo, nigga you can take you and that bullshit your talking and rise the fuck up out of my crib! Nigga you don't know shit about grieving! Bitch you're the reason why my brother is dead!

You introduced us to this bullshit lifestyle and it got my brother murdered! Man, I don't want to hear shit you got to say. On the real. Now step nigga! Get the fuck out of my house before I do something I might regret!" I snapped as Monika grabbed ahold of my arm.

Black didn't say a word. He just turned heading to the door. It was hard not to hate that motherfucker right now man. I didn't give a fuck if he was my father.

"I came over here so we could plan your brother's funeral. Listen, kid I made my share of mistakes but you and Reggie are still my sons. The only mistakes I didn't make were having you two. Hate me if you wanna but it's not going to take the pain away. I'll be at the funeral home tomorrow making arrangements. If you want to join me I would love to have you there son." He stated before disappearing. That nigga was good for that shit...

I sat back in my chair continuing to roll up an L as Monika came and sat on my lap combing her first gets through my hair that needed to be braided.

"Honey, I know the last thing you want to hear is that I'm sorry but I am babe. I am sorry that I can't take this hurt and pain out of your heart. It pains me to see you hurting like this. But..." She started as I cut in.

"Big 9 is missing." I said.

"What the fuck you mean my cousin is missing Ace? Did you check the old hang out spot?" She panicked jumping up off if my lap.

"Bae, I checked everywhere. Every spot no one seen him. That nigga would've never missed seeing Reggie before he took his last breath. On the real ma. I think someone did something to him." I admitted.

Monika's face turned up in straight disgust. Right then I didn't know what was going through her mind and to be honest, I didn't want to know either.

Ignoring the outside world for just a second, I lit my 'L' hoping to get a piece of mind. That shit lasted less than a minute.

"What the fuck?"

I could hear Monika in the back room crying. Damn, I hated that I had to tell shorty that but she needed to know.

After taking a deep sigh, I took another pull from my blunt before putting it out. I have to go and check on Monika.

When I entered our bedroom, she was on the bed with her face in the pillow. She continued to sob softly.

"Mo, listen ma. I promise you with everything in me that I am going to find out where Big 9 is alright? I got you." I promised.

She lifted her head up looking at me. I sat on the bed beside her as she sat straight up.

"Thank you Ace. Just please don't do anything stupid babe. Oh, and I really do think that you need to help your father plan Snake's funeral." She added as she leaned in kissing my lips softly.

I could feel my dick as is nudged through my clothes. Damn, baby girl had a way with that tongue to make a nigga hunger for her body. It was like a crackhead needing crack and not being able to get the shit.

Monika's body was my crack though and I was about to smoke it up. I was ready to get high...

Standing up, Monika strutted in front of me and threw her legs across mine. She then gently took a seat on my erect dick as she whispered in my ear.

"I want you to make love to me." She begged as I lifted her up and matched her thrust.

That shit right there! It was about to make me explode too fucking fast. I had to switch shit up.

Laying her soft body down on the bed, I leaned over her and kissed her soft cherry red lips. Moving down to her neck, I listened to her soft moans. They sounded like music to my ears. Next, I unbuttoned her shirt taking my time to grace her stomach with my lips.

"Mmmmmm" she purred.

I reached behind her back unlatching her bra. I was instantly memorized by her big DDD breasts with her perfectly round hard nipples that stood at attention. They were just waiting on me to put them in my mouth and suck on them like I was getting nursed.

I caressed one breast while sucking on the other as she pulled my hair. She drew it in a downward direction. I followed her lead and moved down licking every inch of baby girls' body. Including her lips and I didn't mean the ones on her face either. Her pussy was so juicy, wet and it smelled like peaches and cream. Umm my favorite. Just the way that daddy liked it.

I just had to go down and taste her. When I did, juices poured out like a bucket over flowing with nothing but my tongue to clean it up. The louder she moaned the more I was certain that I was hitting her favorite spot. I had her ass right where I wanted her.

"Come on daddy put that dick back inside of me." She moaned and bit her lip.

Monika was urging for daddy to fuck the shit out if her. Trust me, that was just what I was about to do. Her wish was my command.

I quickly pulled my boxers all the way off. They were tearing up the circulation around my calves. When I made it back onto the bed, Monika climbed right back on top.

While she kissed my lips, she placed my dick in the proper position and sat right on it once again. "Damn!" I began to moan as she moved her body up and down. To gain a rhythm, I grabbed ahold of her waist but that shit was too much.

Quickly flipping her over, Monika got on all fours. That was when I went in for the kill. I was pounding hard on that ass as she screamed out my name.

"That's right baby. Let me hear you scream out for me." I thought in my head as I went faster.

"Oh shit, baby you know you got me ready to... I'm about to... Damn, I'm cumming!" she screamed as I continued pounding that ass.

I couldn't stop. I hadn't gotten my shit off yet.

"Give me 5 more seconds' babe." I requested biting my lips as I released.

I rolled over lying flat on my back as she kissed my lips. When she drew back, she stretched out and laid her head on my chest. I rubbed her back and told her that I loved her.

The exceptional sexual getaway was cool, but it was only temporary. I thought I would feel better but I didn't.

The thought of seeing Reggie laying there lifeless continued to play in my head. It was like a record that played over and over on repeat. It was like dealing with G-Mom's death all over again.

I didn't know if I could handle it again. One thing I did know though. I was about to end HB and his whole team that he called himself getting together.

Ain't no damn way that nigga is gonna be King of East Harlem. Mark my motherfucking words.

Chapter Four

Toni

I heard a quote when I was a child that started: "The scars you can't see are the hardest to heal." (Astrid Alauda)

The hardest thing for any mother to do was sit there and watch their child go through what my baby girl was going through. I knew that I had made my share of mistakes but my biggest one was trusting Harlem with my daughter.

At that point in my life I didn't want to raise no baby. I wanted to continue my life as a drug addict and a prostitute. Getting high and fucking random men was all that I wanted until I met Slick Rick. He made me want to change my life around.

By that time I was already pregnant with Kera. I was lucky that Slick Rick was an OG that loved me but unfortunate that he did not love my child cause it was by someone else.

My dumb ass thought by giving Kera to Harlem she would give my baby a chance at a better life but damn was I completely wrong. She allowed my baby to get raped over and over again by that son of bitch ass husband of her that even she was a afraid of. Then she shot my baby and landed her in the hospital fighting for her life.

I kept praying that God would deliver Kera from that coma but I felt that he was not listening to me. Why would he though? Look at all the choices I made. I had a chance to make it right with Kera when she ran away and came to live with me but I didn't. I still chose to allow her to go down the wrong path.

Hell, I still wasn't in the right mind to be a mother then either. I was already used to being her aunt.

"Damn!" Looking at my daughter that way made me sick to my stomach. If I could take her pain away I would.

I continued to hold onto her hand looking down at her lying there helpless. "My baby"

"How is she doing?" A male voice asked.

Turning around, I saw Miguel standing behind me. First thing that went through my head was why in the hell was he there! "What the hell can he possible want?"

"What are you doing here Miguel?" I questioned sitting back in the chair beside my baby.

"Look Toni, I know I made my share of mistakes but I love Kera. I always have since the very first time I saw her when she was walking down the street with you and Slick Rick. May he rest in peace. I remember because she had on a pink t-shirt with the red flowers and butterflies on it. I remember because red roses and butterflies was her favorite. She said it made her feel like she was in a different place with peace. Look Toni I got some shit to tell you."

Just as Miguel began, DMack walked in. His presence stopped him midsentence and he left the room.

"What the hell is this?" I asked myself then spoke on it.

"Alright what the hell is going on?" I questioned as we moved to the corner of the room so Red wouldn't hear shit.

"Look Toni, we need your help to bring HB down. I know about you. Not only was you an addict but once you got clean you was the biggest Queen Pin in Harlem. My pops used to tell me stories about you. You ain't the one to double cross. You're just as bad as that nigga Black." DMack ran down shit.

Silently I wondered how that kid knew more about my past than Red did.

"What the hell do ya want me to do?" I replied getting straight to the point.

"Alright look, HB is planning over to take over the game. He's already taking out people that hold loyalty to Red and Snake. This motherfuckers needs to be stopped." DMack spat.

Everything sounded good, but how did I really know if I could fucking trust that nigga? He was still alive when his ass should have been dead three times over.

"Why are you still alive then DMack and how do I know that I can trust you. See that was the mistake that Red made. She trusted to many motherfuckers that turned around and stabbed her in the back. So forgive me if right now I don't believe a word that comes out your mouth." I said holding back my composure.

"Look Toni, I respect that shit dead ass but I ain't here to hurt Red. I am trying to protect her and Ace. This nigga has it out for them both and anyone that gets in his way. You know what I'm saying. I ain't gonna let no one fuck with Queenie." He guaranteed.

I still found it hard to believe that HB spared his life. I didn't know what the fuck to do. All I knew was that I needed to protect Red. I was going to do everything in my power to make sure no one fucked with mine.

"Look let me handle this shit and don't come back up here bringing that shit around Red. Now get the fuck out. I got some phone calls to make. This motherfucker wants to come for mine. I'm about to show him. Ain't no man gonna hurt mine. It's war time now bitches."

Chapter Five

HB

It was the big day. It was time to meet up with that nigga Kevin to see what was really good. I truly hoped that I didn't have to off that nigga too for staying loyal to Queenie and that bitch ass nigga Snake.

I had heard through the streets that Ace and Black had been planning a nice funeral for that nigga. I guessed that they were trying to send that motherfucker out in a style. That was something that he didn't deserve if you asked me. Shit, if you left that shit up to me, I would have just burnt his fuckin body.

"Fuck this shit. Let me be about my paper!"

I decided to take True and Real with me to meet up with Kevin. I was going to allow those motherfuckers to see how I handled shit. So they knew what was up.

"Yo, tell that nigga Kevin HB is here to see him." I hollered to one of his men that stood outside his fucking door posted up.

Niggas had some fucking protection now. Shit was truly real in the game.

A tall ass nigga came out as the other two niggas stood their post. I could tell he was coming out to talk shit. I was prepared though.

"Yo nigga, Kevin said get the fuck lost. He don't want to see your ass." The nigga clowned as he motioned us to get off his property.

I instantly looked at my crew. They already knew the deal before I said anything.

Simultaneously, we pulled out our pieces and blasted on those niggas. For some reason I knew that Kevin was going to bitch up. I had something for that ass though.

I got out the car walking past his dead homeboys and straight into the house. What I walked in on was something truly disrespectful to the game.

That nigga Kevin was kicked back in the bed while another man sucked on his dick. *These motherfuckers can't be serious.*

I lifted my piece capping that nigga right between the eyes and shooting the other nigga in the back of the head. If he wasn't working for me, he wasn't working for anyone. *Bet that hot shit.*

I grabbed the rest of the supplies that he left lying on the floor beside the bed. Shit from the looks of it he was smoking his own shit.

There was a small piece of aluminum foil and straw sitting on the dresser with coke inside. *Stupid ass motherfuckers how you supposed to be a supplier and you're getting high off your own shit?*

Kevin had left the rest of the goods in a huge black duffle bag on the floor. I scooped that up and the money that he had in his closet.

There was not only one, but there were several duffle bags full of money. *Kevin should of never shown niggas where he kept his shit.*

I ran to the car and tossed the duffle bags in the back seat as we sped off. Now I had to find another connect, but at least I would be straight until then.

By the looks of the come up, Kevin must have just re-upped. That made it perfect to set shit up. It would look like two crackheads were killed over some drugs. No one ever solved those types of murders around there.

I didn't like that bitch anyway. Boy I'll tell you what, Queenie had a crazy ass way of finding motherfuckers, but I had a crazy ass way of getting rid of them too.

"Yo, HB what the fuck are we gonna do with all this shit cuz?" True asked as we pulled into a parking garage a couple of blocks away from the scene.

Black's punk ass always taught us to have a plan B so trust a nigga like me always had one.

"Grab the bags and come on. Nigga like me stays prepared for shit like this." I assured getting out the car looking around for a nice whip to jack.

I reached into my pocket grabbing my black gloves. I put them on and continued to look for the right car. It didn't take me long before I spotted it.

There it was, a black 2016 BMW 535i. Hell yeah. That was the shit that I fucking needed. Shit was fit for a King.

"This is what I want and y'all niggas are going to be the ones to bring it to me." I ordered as Real walked to the trunk looking for something to unlock the door with.

As we approached the car you could hear someone treading through the garage. We hopped in and got somewhere making the tires squeak as we did so. We exited the garage and sped down the street.

Cops were posted up on each corner trying to send a message but no one paying their lame ass any mind. They knew who ran the streets and I guaranteed that if they didn't then they were going to find out.

"Let me get at everyone."

The only thing left to do was to meet up with the rest of those niggas and get shit popping. I grabbed my phone calling up DMack.

"Yo, nigga meet me at the crib in 15 minutes and tell them other niggas to meet me there too." I commanded hanging up before he could get a word out.

Fifteen minutes passed as we sat in the kitchen bagging up. We had been making use of our time as we waited for those niggas to fucking show up.

Sophia sat in the living room rocking our baby to sleep. Seeing my son grow was such a beautiful thing. Still couldn't believe that the little nigga was a week away from being two.

RJ was everything that I wanted in a little shorty man. Even though he had that bitch ass nigga Reggie's name, he was still my seed.

Everything I do. I do for him.

A knock came the door shaking me from my thoughts. As I rose up to my feet, I walked over to the entrance and peeked out of the hole.

When I stepped back, I looked at Sophia telling her with my eyes. "Get my son the fuck outta here!"

She could tell what that meant and wasted no time in moving her ass. She grabbed RJ, his bottle and carried him off to the back.

When they were out of sight, I looked through the peephole again to make sure it was those niggas. I couldn't believe that they took their own sweet fucking time to show up.

What the fuck? Niggas weren't ever late to Snake nor Queenies meetings and those motherfuckers weren't going to be late for mine. *Fuck out of here.*

"What the fuck took you niggas so long? Motherfucker I said 15 minutes! From now on when I give you a time to be here niggas, y'all be here!" I demanded with a frown.

"Nigga chill shit! The cops are rolling around looking for whoever popped that nigga Kevin and some nigga that had his dick in his mouth. Word around town is that faggot ass nigga got taken out for smoking his suppliers shit. I never thought that this nigga was smoking that shit cuz."

That nigga DMack ran down the whole spill. The streets were talking and I had to be on top of my game in order to keep shit under my control.

"I heard that shit too. That shit is unbelievable kid. I never thought that shit either fam. I bet Queenie didn't know that shit cause if she did she would have never made that fucking fruitcake as our connect." I acknowledged.

I could tell that those niggas already knew that I popped his sorry ass. When DMack said it I felt my cheeks rise. I tried to suppress my grin but I couldn't. That gay as motherfucker had it coming.

"So what's up nigga?" DMack said sitting down at the table as Real and True continued to bag up.

He just sat there and watched me school my niggas. They knew the drill but I was just adding emphasis on the shit to show DMack that I knew what I was doing.

"Alright look, these are my niggas Real and True. They are our new baggers and they collect all the money from you and your workers and bring it to me. I want up to control all of East Harlem. Every block, every corner, everything. We ain't leaving shit for anyone else. If anyone gets in your face about it, don't hesitate to take their ass out. So get some product and get out there fuck outta here and do what you need to do." I demanded.

My workers each grabbed some shit and headed out the door. Now my crew was ready for the takeover.

Chapter Six

Ace

The dreadful day had finally arrived that I had to see my brother off. I honestly still couldn't believe that Snake was gone man.

I kept going over the nightmare in my head thinking that I would wake up from it, but I couldn't. It wasn't a dream...

Reality will kick in today I guess.

The night before, I had spent the night in the hospital. I was watching over Queenie. I was talking to her about everything that was going on right then.

Shit still didn't look promising for her, but me and Toni were holding out on faith that she would pull through it. I never thought in a million years that I would have to deal with that much pain all at once.

That wasn't the only thing that was bothering me. There was still no word on Big 9. I honestly was starting to think that my nigga was dead.

Monika had got in contact with his mom and they went to the police station to do a missing person report. I didn't see why they even bothered knowing that those motherfucking crooked ass cops wasn't looking for him. They thought that he was just another hustler that was killed for some bullshit ass beef in the streets. They didn't know Big 9 like I did though.

I definitely knew that he would never pull a 'no show'. In all the years that we had been friends with Snake Big 9 would have not missed his funeral. That was shit our bro just wouldn't do.

I think that bitch ass nigga HB has something to do with it.

Monika walked in the room right in time to distract me. She was wrapped in a towel and looking sexy as ever.

Stepping over to the mirror, I fought to fix my tie. When I looked up, I saw Monika's face in the reflection. It was all lit up like she had just gotten some good news or something.

Shit, right then I could have used some good news. I wanted desperately to get my mind off of saying goodbye to my brother.

"Babe, how are you holding up?" Monika asked as she began to help me out. "Stand still babe. I will fix it for you."

"Thanks baby."

"You know, I can't really imagine what you are feeling right now, but later I have something to tell you. Right now I want you to deal with this."

"Okay baby, that's cool. Just know if you need to talk I'm here."

"I know Ace and I love you. We will get through this together. I promise." She said as she kissed me on my lips before heading to the bed to get ready.

I walked over to my side of the bed looking on my nightstand. I located my small tin 49ers can which hold my eight dime bags inside. I grabbed and the pineapple game wrap that laid beside my tin can. *Shit, as hard as this day is going to be a nigga need to blow down a fat ass L.*

I mean especially since I had to deal with all the fake ass motherfuckers who were coming to my brother's funeral. I was talking those same fools that never truly gave a fuck about him.

I'm including aunts, uncles and fucking cousins a nigga never knew that he had.

Black was the kind of man who made his family hate the ground that he walked on. His family hated his ass for all the choices that he continued to make.

Even Snake's grandma on his mother side was coming. Last time I heard she hadn't seen him since he had been born. Now she wanted to show her face because my brother is gone.

See that was the fake shit that I was talking about. Damn, I hoped that I could compose myself. I didn't want to have to fuck someone up for disrespecting my brother. On the real.

As I rolled my blunt, my mind ran across Red. The last time she had a funeral for Snake that shit almost destroyed her. That shit happened only for us to find out that he was still alive. Now he was really gone and she was in a coma and wouldn't ever be able to say her goodbyes. *I'm telling you man shit is fucked up.*

My phone rang taking me out my thoughts. It was Toni. My heart pounded rapidly as I answered.

"What's up Toni?" I greeted as I lit my blunt.

I took a drag as I prepared myself. I didn't know if I was about to get good or bad news.

"I was calling to tell you. Red's heart completely stopped. They had to perform CPR. They did manage to bring her back. They had to put her in a medical induced coma. They are telling me that she might not wake up. They are actually talking to me about taking her off of life support. They want me to let my baby die Ace. What the fuck am I going to do?" she cried.

"Listen, I will be up there after Snake's funeral. Don't make no decisions until I get there." I suggested.

"Alright." she agreed as I hung up.

I took a long drag of my blunt. I swear man if it wasn't one thing it was another. Now it was Queenie. *What the fuck?*

Monika entered back into the room after fixing her makeup in bathroom.

"Ace, honey what's wrong?" she questioned.

I held back my tears as the limo beeped its horn. Damn, my worst fears were about to come true. Shit, it felt kind of weird being dressed in a suit and tie but a nigga had to have a fresh pair of J's on to match.

Shit, my brother always told me said if something ever happened to him to wear a suit and a fresh pair of J's to his funeral. That was just what I wore.

"I always got you bro." I said to myself as I took Monika's hand.

As we headed out the house, I threw on my black shades to hide the tears in my eyes. That was maybe one of the hardest days of my life.

I was almost to the car when my phone went off. *Who the fuck could this be?*

"Who the fuck is this?" I asked listening closely to try and figure out who the fuck it was calling me.

"Yo, Ace listen kid. Someone offed that nigga Kevin. He was found in his house with a bullet in his head right along with his partner. Kid, shit is real in the game." the person said hanging up.

What the fuck? Damn, shit is fucked up in game right now.

How the fuck did someone off the connect? It had to be HB's doing right there. The only nigga I knew that would do something like fucking off the damn connect was that stupid fool. That nigga didn't want anyone who was connected to Red or Snake breathing. That nigga wanted to knock everyone off. Now it was his turn.

HB thought that my brother was bad, but he had no idea about me and how I fucking gave it up.

Fake ass motherfucker going to see, just watch...

Chapter Seven

Toni

Seeing my daughter like that pissed me off, but not as much as hearing about niggas dirty-macking her name in the streets did. They thought that just because I got out the game so long ago that I couldn't make a phone call and get shit popping.

Newsflash! I could shut HB's shit down by dialing one number. Everyone respected my hubby Slick Rick and everyone knew about me. Shit, back in the day I was known for cutting a niggas dick off and feeding it to him for coming for me and mine. After I did that shit they stayed clear. Once Slick Rick was murdered I stopped that shit.

I had it going on until I broke the golden rule. That was one thing you wasn't ever supposed to do in the game. Smoke your own shit.

I even stopped selling it so that I could get high. I was depressed with the life that I was forced to live after they took Slick from me. My whole life had shattered into pieces and there was no way of fixing it. Just like then, my life was shattering once again.

One moment I was looking at my daughter full of life and the next I was watching her slip away before my very eyes. It was an unbearable pain that words couldn't even describe. I keep telling myself it would get better but I knew it wouldn't.

Miguel hadn't left Red side since she flatlined. He had only left to let me talk business. He was right back ten minutes later.

"Toni how is she doing?" a familiar voice asked.

I glance behind me to see HB standing in the doorway. I really didn't have shit to say to him.

"What the hell do you want HB? I heard you took over the streets. Congratulations kid but you still aint shit. You think cause Snake is gone and my child is laying up in here you can run East Harlem. Let's see how long that shit will last. These streets will eat a little pussy ass motherfucker like you up quicker than you think."

"You think so?"

"Yeah, aint no one in the game got respect for a nigga that aint loyal to his crew. Streets talk nigga and I know all about you." I smirked looking him up and down.

"Yeah i know about you too. You aint shit like you seem to think Toni. What you are is a used to be Queen Pin that got addicted to her own shit. You was the real reason why Slick Rick got popped. They was coming to kill your ass and that nigga got in the way."

"Is that the story you're spreading cause I aint heard no shit like that!" I spat with venom.

"Bitch you aint shit and if you keep coming for me I'm gonna do what those others niggas couldn't."

"Oh yeah, and what's that?"

"I will take you and Red out. Try me bitch." he threatened.

HB must have thought that his threat hurt me but that shit rolled off like oil. Shit, I knew for a fact that he was not going to do shit to me or my daughter.

"Yo, kid I thought I told your ass not to come around here. I guess I ain't made that shit clear last time. Stay the fuck away from Queenie. This is the last time that I warn your ass." Ace spat as he entered Red's room wearing a suit and tie.

He was holding tightly onto Monika's hand. It was kind of like he was protecting her. I could tell from his face he wasn't with HB's bullshit.

"Your shorty looking really good today," HB flirted while playing Ace real close. "Ma, you need to come on over here to a real nigga and leave that clown ass nigga right where he stands." he spat disrespectfully.

Ace's face turned blood shot red. Next his fist balled up.

"Nigga what?" Ace yelled out as he began charging at HB.

I had to step in between. We were in Red's room.

"Hell no. We aint going to do this shit in here. Ace, stay in here with Red. Let me handle this shit with HB." I stated as we both stepped out into the hallway.

"What you want bitch?" he spat jumping right up in my face.

"Count your days because those motherfuckers are numbered. You threaten me and mine bitch I will make you a promise."

"What the fuck can you promise me old crack head bitch?" HB snapped with spit flying out of his mouth.

"You will be dead soon. Mark my fucking word." I spoke calming before walking back into my daughter's room then closing the door behind me.

That sorry ass fool didn't have a chance to say a word. Once he saw I was serious and security crept up behind him, that nigga got the message.

"Ace, I'll be back." I said grabbing up my jacket heading out the door. I had to leave after that shit with HB. There was no way that I was about to take his threat lightly. I was going to show him just how I responded to shit like that.

"Time to go make a couple rounds." I said preparing myself mentally for what was about to happen.

I left the hospital and decided to take a stroll down to the old neighborhood to see what was going on. I hadn't been on them in a minute, but folks knew me.

Damn, these streets ain't even the same anymore. Slick Rick used to hold shit together. Those niggas out there now didn't know shit about the game but I knew one hustler that did.

"Yo ma, what the fuck? Tee, ma what the fuck are you doing here? Man, I haven't seen your ass in a while." TBone said as I walked up.

Man, the last time I saw that nigga was at Slick's funeral. Yeah, it had been a while.

"I know I've been on the low, but shit is real in the streets right now. You heard about that new cat HB who's trying to take over EH." I began.

"Damn, there's a new one? I heard about that nigga Snake and then some chick name Red. Now who is this new nigga. What the fuck happened to the other two?" he asked.

I guessed right away that Slick never told TBone about Red. Everyone knew that I had a daughter but no one knew it was Red until recently.

"Well, that nigga Snake is dead and Red is in a coma. Before you ask how I know, Red is my daughter. No, she's not Slick's."

"Oh, okay."

"Now, back to business," I sighed. "I need you to send a message to this cat HB. You know the way that we used to do it? He threatened me and mine. I need the message the he gets to be loud and motherfucking clear." I instructed with a straight face.

"No doubt about it ma. I got you T. No one fucks with Slick's peeps and gets away with it. That's on my hood."

"Thanks TBone," I replied.

"I'll hit you when it's done." he guaranteed.

I knew that if anyone could relay a physical message it was TBone. That fool was no joke in the streets. He had come through for me and Slick more times than I could remember. He never let us down.

I wanted HB so bad I could taste it. That shit was foul flavored too...

Nigga wanna to play? Cool let's play, but bet I will be the one on top when the dust settles.

Chapter Eight

Ace

After leaving the hospital, it was time to head to the funeral and I was already in my emotions. "Damn, I hate this shit."

While pulling up to the church, I could feel my heart fall to my knees. Maybe it was the fact of knowing that my brother was lying in a casket at the front of this church.

I grabbed Monika's hand as I stepped out of the limo. My chest was pounding rapidly.

I gripped her hand tighter as Black stepped into the limo behind us. He was with Snake's grandma Mary and her new husband. Some clown ass nigga that no one ever met.

I held my composure as Monika tapped me on my arm. When I faced her, she just smiled.

"Are you ready to do this son?" Black asked as I held back from telling him what I really wanted to say. So I just did the right thing and didn't say shit at all.

That day was about Snake not that clown ass nigga Black. I chose to ignore him as best as I could.

That was the first time that I got to see my brother seen he had passed. I couldn't go to the wake. I couldn't do it and listen to all those fake motherfuckers cry and scream over someone that they didn't really know. That shit would have just pissed me off more than anything.

Clinching on to Monika's wrist, we headed into the church. You would never think that you would be prepared for something like that.

My heart dropped as I opened the doors of the church. With little hesitation, Monika and I walked down to the altar where the brushed light gold casket with Tiger Eye shade ebony finish was positioned. It had a beige velvet interior with his name engraved inside. I was surprised the casket was even opened. I had to peek at my brother's resting body.

Tears begin to roll down my face as Monika grabbed ahold of my arm. My whole body became numb. It was like I wanted to move but couldn't.

Suddenly I felt an arm on my other shoulder. "Yo, it's okay bro. We are gonna get through this. You gotta strong bro."

It was DMack and his words broke me down. That let loose the waterworks for real.

Monika and DMack were both holding onto me as they escorted me to my seat. *I never thought in a million years I would ever picture my brother like this man.*

Sometimes I thought about all the times that we shared. I was wishing that we could get it back but I knew we couldn't. That time had come and gone.

"Yo, ya'll up in here moaning over a motherfucker that sold fucking drugs. Are you serious? This nigga is the reason that one of my best friends is dead. This motherfucker sold my boy some drugs and he OD'd. Fuck this nigga man." Some loud mouth motherfucker blurted out.

"Who the fuck is this little nigga man?"

"Ace, babe calm down." Monika pleaded as I rose to my feet.

"This nigga better show my brother some fucking respect!" I whispered becoming irate.

"Yo, son you better show my brother some respect before I make you!" I threatened while rushing at that nigga. My pops grabbed me before I could reach him. He then forced me in a chair.

"Who the fuck this nigga think he is coming up in here disrespecting my motherfucker brother? Nigga lucky we are in a church and I don't have my piece cause he would have gotten a hot one. I ain't playing!" I huffed silently.

Niggas always wanted to blame somebody for somebody else's shit. I couldn't understand it.

Lucky I didn't have to remove that trouble maker from the church. I got the pleasure of watching someone else grab that big mouth fool and carry his ass outside. That nigga was still yapping.

DMack and Monika walked over to me as soon as Black left my side. They tried to calm me down, but what I really wanted do was go outside and beat the fuck out that big mouthed ass motherfucker.

I looked up at my brother's casket as I calmed myself down. The last thing I wanted to do is disrespect Snake.

I got up heading to the front row as Mary grabbed my arm. I really wanted to ask her what the fuck was she doing there. She never gave a damn about Snake nor Pam. Now she wanted to sit there and act like she cared about my brother.

"I'm sorry Ace." she apologized.

"Don't say sorry to me. Say sorry to my brother who is stretched out in that casket. You disowned him not me." I reminded as she released my arm. When she did, I returned to my seat.

Her guilt was something she had to live with not me. She chose not to be a part of my brother's life. She had many chances but I guess the way that she felt about Pam kept her from her grandson. Now she wanted to sit up here and cry.

Too late for that fake shit. You should have cherished him when he was alive.

We left the church and then came the hardest part. That was watching them close my brother's casket and lower it into the ground. That shit right there let me know he was gone forever. I never imagined it would be so painful, but it was.

After we left the cemetery, I thought about heading up to the hospital to check on Queenie. With everything that was going on, the doctors wanted to tell Toni to take Queenie off life support.

Hell no. She is going to fight and come back to us. She is strong. She ain't going to leave us yet.

Well at least I hoped not.

Making my way up to Queenie's room I saw that bitch ass nigga HB up there again. *"Come on son you can't be serious. How many times do I have to tell this nigga to stay the fuck away from Red?"*

I guess that nigga had to learn the hard way...

Chapter Nine

HB

'Who the fuck do these niggas think that they are?' I asked myself as I headed out the hospital doors before I shook shit the fuck up.

Toni was lucky I had compassion for her cracked out ass. The only thing that was saving her ass was the connection she had with Slick.

Everyone feared Slick because they knew if they crossed him or came for him what would happen. Shit, nigga was no fucking joke. He was one of the old cats that showed Black the ropes. Shit, you would never tell from how that nigga Black ain't shit cuz. I mean look at Snake and Ace.

When I got in the car, I got a call telling me that Ace and his boys gave that bitch ass nigga Snake a heartfelt and touching ass funeral and shit. They said the Black had to hold that nigga Ace back from fucking up a couple of his kin folks for talking shit about that nigga Snake. Yo man that nigga had it all and appreciated nothing. Now he was gone.

Honestly he got exactly what he had coming. Nigga cheated on Queenie, fucked over Sophia and fucked up our whole fucking crew.

I knew that nigga Ace wasn't taking shit to well, but coming for me was only creating more problems for the nigga. He was going to be the next one that Black had to bury if he didn't watch himself.

Back on the streets my niggas True, Real, DMack, Trigga, and ZMoney starting shit off right. Niggas was already hating cause they know that me and my niggas were taking over.

We were changing the rules of the game, one street corner at time. We had niggas hating from a distance but a motherfucker like me didn't give a fuck as long as they realized who the king was.

We will shut anybody down that steps this way including Toni, Ace, Miguel, and even Red. If she every wakes up.

On the real I hoped she didn't cause I would really hate to take her out too. Shit, don't get me wrong. Queenie, had been really good to me, but now it was my time to shine. Loyalty was the last thing on my mind.

To be honest my loyalty never lied with Red nor Snake. A nigga like me was and always would be loyal to the game and that was it. Shit, that's how I was taught to play the game.

ROC showed me that you had to play the game to win. He said that sometimes you even had to play both sides until you were the last one standing.

As you can see I am the last one to play the game.

Snake was dead, ROC was dead and Red was on her way out the door herself. Those niggas thought that Ant was the one that couldn't be trusted and it was me all along. I got that nigga killed and I knew just what to do. Now I was just where I wanted to be. The top. The new and better King of East Harlem.

I posted up on the wall as the fiends ran up ready to get a fix. My eyes were glued on a beautiful diamond in the ruff as she walked her fine ass down the street. She was dressed just like I liked her. She sported some skin tight jeans with a hot pink halted top shirt and a hot fresh pair of J's. Looking good as fuck. Damn, she made me want to take her around the corner and stick this dick in every spot that had an opening. *If you know what I mean?*

"What's up ma?" I greeted Sophia kissing her soft ass lips.

A Silver 2015 BMW with dark black tinted windows rolled up slowly. That caught my full attention.

I grabbed Sophia's arm shoving her into the alley. Those niggas were there for one thing and one thing only, a fucking Drive-By!

I pulled out my 9mm as soon as I saw the back window roll down. That nigga started blasting off immediately.

Before I could think twice, I fired back while ducking beside the mail box filled with dirty ass needles from those nasty ass drug-heads. I prayed that I didn't get stuck with any of them.

As the car made it halfway down the block, I ran in the middle of the street and began blasting off. I could hear the niggas screaming out as they continued to drive away.

"Stay the fuck away from Lady T!" They yelled as they turned the corner sharply.

I turned back looking at one of my niggas as they laid face down on the ground. He was soaked in blood and there wasn't shit I could for his ass but call the ambulance or coroner.

Sophia rushed out. She was alright but I examined her anyway as she ran into my arms.

For a moment I thought I lost her. I kissed her lips before running over to Trigga's side. I knew once I saw him that he was gone.

"Damn, all this over a bitch name Lady T? Who the fuck is Lady T?"

Just then I remembered that it was what that bitch Toni used to go by back in the fucking day. That bitch was becoming a major fucking problem that I really didn't need right then.

I couldn't believe that the stupid bitch sent some punk ass niggas after my crew causing one of my niggas to be shot. Trigga was my nigga…

"Yo HB, nigga we need to get Trigga to the hospital. This nigga ain't doing too good over here. Nigga are you going coming we need to go now." DMack spat.

I nodded and looked over at my shorty. Yes, Sophia was scared out of her fucking mind.

"Y'all niggas go ahead. I'm gonna take wifey home. Meet y'all up there." I told them as I went to hold Sophia.

I held on to her as we watched True and Real pick up Trigga and put him into the backseat. I escorted wifey to the car and placed her inside.

"Damn, this dumb bitch Toni is making enemies where she don't need them."

When I began to pull from the curb, DMack sped down the street trying to get Trigga to the hospital. Honestly, the way shit looked, that nigga was already gone.

I drove off as tears poured down Sophia's face. That life wasn't built for her. She wanted to act all hard and shit but she wasn't.

I probably was the one who turned her into the monster she thought she was, but she still had that weak ass side to her.

That bitch was so in love with Snake that I had to make her into what I wanted her to be and it still didn't do shit. She still wasn't no Red, I'll tell you that.

Sophia would never be able to hold down the game like Queenie did. The game would destroy her way worse and quicker than what I could.

"Yo, what the fuck are you crying for? This shit is a part of the game. Niggas get hurt. This is what fucking happens ma. Niggas get shot. They die. It's all how the game is played. Queenie ain't never cried over this shit." I clowned as Sophia hurried to dry those unnecessary tears.

"Motherfucker don't you ever. I betrayed her trust for your ass. I sent Harlem after her because you said so and you're gonna try to play me. I could've had your ass taken out a long time ago. I know all your dirt HB, all of it. So don't try me with what Red will or won't do bullshit cause I ain't her." She snapped sounding beyond pissed off.

"Bitch, please aint none of these motherfuckers gonna believe you, especially now that they know that you ain't nothing but a fucking slut that goes from hustler to hustler. Fuck outta here with that bullshit bitch." I huffed. Soon as I released those words I felt a cold crisp slap come across my face.

"I really fuckin hate you HB." Sophia cried as I leaned in and tried to kiss her to calm her down.

She tried to fight it but I knew she wanted me just as much as I wanted her. Talking shit to her turned me on. No matter what anyone said, Sophia was my ride or die bitch. She was the only bitch that was ever truly down for me.

Thinking she was going to try something, I quickly pulled off on the side of a back street. I had to see where her head was.

"What's up?" I asked while I slid my seat back.

Sophia climbed over onto my lap. She grabbed the knife out of my arm rest and cut a hole into her jeans right between her legs. I could see right away that she was not wearing any underwear. That was my cue to unzip my pants and retrieve my long hard big dick.

Sophia licked the palm of her hand as she grabbed a hold of my dick. She jerked it just a little before climbing onto it. I removed her halter as I studied her perfect size breast.

As I pulled her in closer, I licked around her soft nipples before I began nursing like a starving baby. "Mmmmmm"

She went up and down while bouncing her big ass on my dick. Next, she began to sing sweet tones as the warmest of her juices trickled down.

Just before I could reach my climax, Sophia climbed off of my dick and slid it into her mouth. I immediately dipped my head and bit down on my finger as she went to work.

She was doing things that she never did before. She was sending a nigga to a place that not even a crack head could make me come back from. *Damn, baby girl sho' got a way with her tongue.*

"Oh fuck!" I shouted as I released all in her mouth. She swallowed then sat back in the seat and fixed herself up.

Right as I gained my composure and started the car, the phone rang. It was that nigga Smack.

"What nigga?" I snapped angry about getting disturbed.

"Yo, nigga you need to get here now. They saying shit ain't looking too good right now for Trigga." He explained in a panic.

Hell, I already knew that shit by the way he was when I glanced over at him lying on the ground. "Alright nigga. I'm on my way." I replied before disconnecting the call.

When I did, I glanced over at wifey. She seemed upset all over again.

"Just drop me off at the house. I know my mom has had enough of RJ by now."

I agreed and got my keys. We headed straight to the car.

That was the shit that I hated. If the nigga was going to die then he was going to die. Why the fuck did we all need to be up there when he took his last motherfucking breath?

Snake was the nigga that always did that shit. He would always be there to hold a niggas hand while they make that last transition but that shit wasn't me. We all came in the world alone and that was the way that shit was when it was time to leave this motherfucker.

I pulled up at the crib as shorty started out the car. She turned back looking at me.

"Be careful. Please come back to your son and I. Shit is real in the game right now and I don't want to lose you too." She said with water in her eyes.

Damn, sometimes I wondered why she loved me. I really wasn't shit except for just another hustler dedicated to the game.

I looked at Sophia for a minute before I drove off. I prayed that her and my son would stay safe.

After leaving there, I headed up to the hospital. When I got there, I parked and went in through the main entrance. That was when my cell rang.

"What the fuck does this nigga want now?"
I thought to myself as I picked it up.

"Nigga I am walking in now. What the hell is
it?"

"Trigga didn't make it nigga. The bullet
pierced his lungs. He died in surgery. Nigga his
mom just came in and she ain't taking this shit well.
Nigga you need to come talk to her." He suggested.

The last thing I wanted to do was to talk to
that niggas family. I wasn't good at that shit.

What made it so hard was that the nigga
had a baby on the way. How could I explain that
shit to his mother let alone his baby mama?

*This bitch done started a war that her ass
can't finish.*

When I got to the emergency unit, DMack,
Real and True were standing outside the room
door. I could hear his mom screaming as I walked
up. I sucked it up and entered into the room. Right
as I did, I viewed Trigga's baby mama and his
mother flipping the hell out.

"I am so sorry for your loss." I said as his mother turned to me and slapped me across the face.

"You all are all alike. My son wanted to turn his life around and leave that street shit alone. After Reggie died that shit almost killed him. Then here you come. I heard about you HB. You are the true snake that everyone needs to beware of. Stay the fuck away from me and my family. If it wasn't for you my son would still be here. You're just as responsible as the men who pulled the trigger. Now leave. Get out and don't come back around here!" Trigga's mother demanded.

I didn't say shit. I just turned my ass around and left the room.

"What do you want to do HB?" True questioned.

"Y'all niggas go get a drink or something we will meet up later. Got something I need to do." I said as we departed. I took the elevator up to Queenie's room. I got off the elevator as Ave and Toni got onto the other one. They didn't see me. They must be heading to get some lunch or something. I headed down the hallway to the private room that Ace and DMack pay for so

Queenie could have her own space to recover. But I
doubt if she is every really going to recover. I stood
at the doorway as the nurse wiped her down.
Damn, I do hate seeing her like this. It's sad where
life takes you sometimes because you chose to love
someone that is dedicated to the streets. Life is full
of surprises I guess. You never know what part of
the stick you're going to get. The nurse turned
around walking to the door closing it. I heard Toni
getting of the elevator as I turned and left. I would
hate to kill this bitch right here and now. Her time
is coming. Sooner than she know.

Chapter Ten

Miguel

The streets weren't even the same anymore since Red had been in a coma. Niggas were acting like loyalty didn't exist anymore. Niggas turned on the one person that had their back with never thinking that in a matter of seconds you could lose that person for good.

Shit, I couldn't lie as if I didn't feel the pain myself because I was just as guilty as the next person. I turned my back on Red when she needed me the most. Maybe I was too afraid that I would turn out not to be the man that she wanted or saw herself with late at night in her dreams.

Now I had to deal with living without her if it came down to it. *Man, fuck the game all I want is her.*

Sometimes you never knew how much a person meant to you until you were forced to let them go. That was something that I refused to do. Losing her would be worse than losing myself.

My grandmother always told me when I found that one woman that I couldn't live without to never give up trying to get her heart. Damn, man if I knew then what I know now I would have made her my wife.

Red was everything that I imagined my wife to be. She was loyal, faithful and smart with a beautiful heart. Even though she had been through hell she was still a rare gem.

I sat in the chair beside Red's bed watching her as she lied there peacefully. I couldn't find the strength to leave her not even for a second because I didn't want to take the chance of not being there if she woke up.

"Red, if you can hear me it's Miguel again. I want you to know that I have been sitting here with you every day. Come back to me Red. Please. I know that there is a lot that you don't trust about me but baby girl trust me when I say that I love you. I know we had a chance a long time ago and I fucked that up but I'm here now. I need for you to fight. You got to fight. Please don't leave me. Please." I pleaded in a whisper as I wiped away the tears that rolled down my cheek.

I guess I now knew what true love felt like. Red was the one for me. She was the only woman that could mend this heart of mine. She did before when my mother used to come in high and beat me.

Red was the one person's shoulder that I could always lean on. I knew if no one else understood what I was going through, I knew she did. She put the sparks in my life the first time that we made love.

Hell, the first time that I saw her I knew she was going to be my wife. Damn, it was amazing how time and plans change.

"Miguel, go home and get some sleep. If anything changes I will call you." Toni promised as she approached me from behind and placed her hand on my shoulder.

"Na, man I can't leave her." I sniffled as Ace and his girlfriend walked into the room right after Toni.

"Look nigga you're lucky to be here in the first place cause I don't trust you and I damn sure don't trust you around Queenie but i ain't going to go there. Toni said that we will call you if anything changes. Now raise the fuck up out of here so I can have time with my sister in law. Alright partner." Ace snapped.

I didn't blame the little nigga for not trusting me but he really had no idea of the shit that I was capable of.

I wasn't going to jump bad there. I wasn't there to try to hurt Red. I just wanted her to know that I was right beside her and that I loved her.

"Yo, look nigga I know you might think you know what is good for Red, but you don't. I didn't come here with no ulterior motives shit. I came for Red. You may not like it Ace and that's cool, but I still think I have the right to be." I said.

That nigga Ace really thought that he put fear in me but he didn't. Not by a long shot...

If he knew what was good, he would get on my page so that he could find out what that nigga HB was up too. I knew more about that niggas plan than Ace did.

"Nigga i don't give a fuck about that shit. I know that my brother didn't trust you and neither do I. You think you got something that's not there anymore. Let go Miguel and move on nigga." Ace huffed just walked off.

The last thing I wanted to do was disrespect Red. I loved her too much to do that. Plus, that nigga Ace really wasn't worth the argument.

Snake didn't trust me because he knew how I felt for Red. He didn't know if Red would choose me or him and now it might be too late for any of us to find out.

Leaving the hospital was the last thing that I ever wanted to do. I kept my cool only because a nigga like me wanted to knock Ace the fuck out. He was damn lucky that Red was lying in that hospital bed because man, if we were on the streets that ass would have been mine.

The minute I exited the hospital doors and made it to the lot, I spotted HB and his punk ass crew leaned all up on my whip.

That bitch ass nigga right there was the last motherfucker that I wanted to deal with.

"What's up you two timing ass bitch?" HB said as I walked up.

"Motherfucker, you don't want it with me. Now take you and your crew and bounce bitch." I spat making them niggas rise up off of my shit.

"Miguel, nigga I think you forgot who the fuck I am kid. ROC ain't even got comfortable in the grave and you're already rolling around with that nigga Black. Talking about loyalty. Red would never be with you nigga so you need to move on and come back and work with me." HB offered.

"Loyalty? Motherfucker you don't know what loyalty is? You want to be rolling with Snake and then when he dies you want to take over the motherfucking game like some motherfucking king killing off your own fucking crew members. Nigga I ain't joining forces with your sorry ass. Fuck outta here. I'll die first bitch." I huffed.

As he took out his piece, I took out mine.

"I think that's what's going to happen then kid."

"You really want to do this nigga?" I asked as someone walked up.

"Drop the weapons now." I twisted around to Black standing there with two 9mm pointed at the both of us.

"What the fuck are you doing here nigga? This here ain't got shit to do with you son." HB said as Black walked up shivering his gun in his face.

His crew knew better than to try Black. They didn't even attempt to pull out their pieces. That nigga Black didn't give a fuck. He would kill all three of those fools with no problem.

Let HB be a dumb motherfucker if he wants. These niggas will be saying RIP to his dumb ass. Let him try Black if he wants to.

"Nigga we can do this the easy way or the hard way. I prefer to do it the easy way but if we have to do it the hard way then that's cool to. Now it's up to you HB or should I say Herbert Brown?" Black said as HB lowered his piece and turned to leave.

When he got a few feet away, he glanced back at Black who still had his piece pointed at him. Without saying a word they hopped into the car and left. Once they drove off, I placed the safety back on my piece and tucked it in the back of my pants.

"What the fuck are you doing here? Still at Red's bedside huh? How is she doing?" He said as we got into the car.

"Not good. Still waiting for her to wake up. Doctors don't think that she is gonna pull through this. What the fuck am I going to do Black? I ain't never felt for no one the way I feel for Red. I fucked up and I know that it is too late to get her back but damn it hurts to know that she is dying and there ain't shit I can do about it! I got another chance to get out this life and damn I thought that it would be spent with her." I said as my eyelids filled up with tears.

"Look Miguel, I can't say that I don't know how you feel. When I first got with Reggie's mom. I felt that same way then I fucked up and she got pregnant. I became a coward running away from my responsibilities. It wasn't until I walked in that house and saw her dead from an OD that I realized that shit. That shit fucking killed me. All I could do was look at my son, at how he just lost his mom and shit. It was hectic. I broke down many nights when I was alone. Let me tell you, you never get over it. You learn how to move on, but the pain doesn't go away. Then, when that shit happens twice you learn to love but to also expect the worst. That's how it is in this life man." Black schooled me.

I tried to understand but I couldn't. All I wanted was for Red to wake up and know that I was still there and how much I loved her.

Man, if she leaves me I don't think that I'll ever be the same.

Chapter Eleven

DMack

Seeing my bro lay in that casket like that began to make me think about my life and how fucking with that nigga HB was going to have me in a casket next. Shit, look what just happened to that nigga Trigga. He was minding his own damn business and got shot a number of times. I mean damn he left behind a family and his girl was pregnant. This shit was real.

You begin to wonder who you could trust in the game. Folks were dying now because of that nigga HB. Dead ass nigga forgot the street rules.

One thing you didn't do was disrespect an OG's family, especially someone like Slick Rick. I mean even dead that nigga got soldiers ready to kill anyone that fucks with his folks. That was just what that dumb ass nigga HB did. He really thought that I was truly on his team but never that.

I was loyal to Snake. He always told me that sometimes you got to play people how they played you. That was just what I was doing to HB.

I had seen on the news the other day that they found a body in the Harlem River. Without the news reporter saying the name I already knew that it was Big 9 that they found. Only one person could be responsible for that punk ass shit.

It was fucked up how HB did that Big 9. He was our brother man. He had a family. He was never supposed to be killed like some punk ass nigga like those two niggas True and Real. I could tell that HB trusted those niggas before he trusted us. We had been there from day one. We were the same ones who knew his strengths and weakness. His brothers man. Or at least that's what i thought.

In all reality, HB was pissed that Big 9 didn't want to be disloyal to Snake. I mean Big 9 was the most kindest, sweetest, nicest motherfucker that you would ever meet. Don't get him fucked up though. He also had that don't fuck with me I'll kill your ass side.

He definitely didn't deserve what he got and neither did Kevin or Trigga, but I guess that was what the game was all about now.

People were killing those who stood in their way of shining. Yeah, I thought it was time to call it quits.

I had to start thinking about my wifey and my kids. The last thing I would ever want was for my boys to grow up and be anything like me. I grew up without my parents and the streets became my pops, my family, my everything...

A lot of shit came along with being a little boy growing up without a pops and in East Harlem. First thing you learn how to do is slang. The fast money, the bitches and the respect is what you get. Everything I needed or wanted I got. Black taught me everything I needed to know and became a father to me.

Shortly after I met my brothers Ty and Snake they became my protectors as I became there's. After Snake lost his mother just like Ty I also became his shoulder to cry on. Some nights after my mother got drunk and forgot I was her son, she tried to have sex with me. I would go to Ty's house where we all would sleep on the floor like brothers. Cause those two nigga were and always will be my brothers.

It pained me that neither of my brothers were there anymore. No one could truly understand the pain that I felt, especially now that Big 9 was gone.

****

Today is my last day in these streets.

They were dead as fuck right then anyway. Not to mention how the police continued to roll through our block every half hour.

HB had made us so hot that the cops wanted to make an arrest every time they suspected that we are up to some shit. No one was fucking safe anymore.

"DMack, let me holla at you for a minute bro." HB said as we walked down the street a little bit.

I didn't know what was going through his mind but whatever it was, I wasn't down.

"What happening?" I asked.

"Look I got a little job for you. I know shit is crazy and all but I hope I can count on you with this request." He started.

"Yeah what's the job?" I inquired patiently waiting for his response.

"I want you to kill that bitch Toni." he requested like it wasn't a big deal.

"Hell no, are you fucking crazy? That's Queenie's mom. Hell no. Find someone else." I snapped with a major attitude.

"Nigga I don't give a fuck whose mother that is. I want that bitch dead and you are going to be the one to do it! That bitch is the reason why Trigga is laying up in the fucking morgue. Fuck outta here. I want that bitch dead. Can I count on you or do I have to go after the ones you love?" HB threatened and placed his hand on my shoulder.

I stood there and fed him the same bullshit that he had been feeding me. That fool must have had lost his fucking mind if he though I was going to allow him to go after mine. Then, think that I was going to go after Queenie's mom?

To top it off, I knew that nigga had something to do with Kevin being murdered. He wanted to play dumb like someone just came up and popped Kevin. Hell na, that nigga Kevin was funny as fuck about who he allowed at his crib and who he showed shit too. I knew it had to be that nigga HB.

Shit, how would anyone else know where that nigga kept all his money? Ain't nobody stupid enough to off Big 9 for being loyal or Kevin for that matter. Who was next, me?

I wasn't worried about shit cause it was about time that I got out of that lifestyle anyways. That shit wasn't cut out for me anymore.

I done lost to many homies to these streets. I want to be a father to my kids and be a better man to my shorty than I have been.

I dapped HB up as I headed down the street. *I guess I better go home first and warn my wifey.* Shit, neither of us had family out there. We needed to get the fuck out of there cause once HB found out that I betrayed him, he was going to try to come after me and my girl. I refused to let that shit happen. I would be damn if he took the only life line that I had left.

"Alright HB. I'll do it." I lied with a straight face.

"That's my nigga. True will go with you." He informed me with a smirk.

What the hell? He thinks I need a fucking bodyguard.

"Na nigga, I got this and plus Toni knows me. She don't know this nigga. She's gonna think something's up." I replied

HB rubbed his perfectly groomed beard and shook his head, "you right. Good thinking my nigga."

"I'm about to head home and change and shit. It will be handled tonight." I bullshitted before heading away.

How the fuck am I going to get Toni away from Red? I don't know how I'm going to pull this shit off.

The last thing I wanted to do was put anybody through any more pain.

"Damn"

I headed down the street towards the apartment building where I've lived. Oddly, I could feel someone following behind me. Damn, it was those niggas True and Real. I knew that shit was going to happen. I knew that HB was going to send some niggas to follow me to make sure that I took Toni out. *He got me fucked up.*

Without warning, I took off running. I found every shortcut I could while trying to lose those two clowns. *I knew it was about to come to this.*

I reached the apartment building with them at least ten steps behind me. I jumped into the elevator as it closed right in time.

What the hell is this? I knew this nigga didn't trust me but damn.

I got off the elevator a floor above mine as I took the stair at the far corner of the hallway down to my floor. I opened the door running into my apartment which was right next to the stairwell.

Soon as I got in, I locked the door. I didn't even see Nicole sneak up behind me. She placed her hands on my shoulder. I jumped and turned to look at her. I then turned back around to peek through the peephole as True and Real passed my apartment with their pieces held out.

I hurried to grab Nicole and pull her into the bathroom. When I closed us in I turned on the shower.

"Are you okay? What the hell have you gotten yourself into Nigel?" She said using my government name.

How do I tell the woman that I love the worst about me? Nicole thinks that I am slanging and that's it. She don't know all the shit that I have to do to take care of her and my sons. Shit ain't easy.

"Look, always know that I love you and my kids and if I die today always remember that."

"I hate it when you talk like that. Ain't nothing going to happen to you. You're going to be fine. We are going to be fine. Stop worrying. If it will make you feel better, I can take the boys and head to my mother's house." She said as I kissed her soft Cherry red lips.

"How did I ever deserve a woman like you? Nicole, Nashawn and NaRon are my world."

The last thing I would ever want was for any motherfucker to think they could target my family. It was time to do what I needed to do.

I took my hoodie out of my closet throwing it on with my black Nets hat on. I walked over to my dresser opening my top draw grabbing both of my fully loaded 9mm. I placed one in my pants and the other in my sock.

"Be careful babe. I love you." She said as I kissed her luscious lips again.

"I love you too. I'll call and check on y'all later." I said heading out of the door.

These clown ass niggas should be gone by now.

I took the stairs to the bottom floor straight out the front door. I didn't know what the fuck I was doing but I knew it was time to tell Ace. He needed to know what the fuck was going on.

Man, it's time to shut this nigga down before he tries to shut us the fuck down.

I snatched up my phone and dialed up Ace as I headed down the streets.

"Yo, nigga I need to meet up with you. Got some shit I need to tell you." I said running across the street.

"Where the fuck are you at motherfucker?" Ace questioned.

I could tell in his voice that he wasn't interested in fucking with none of us right then. Honesty I didn't blame him for how he felt.

"I need you to meet me at Harlem River in fifteen minutes. This shit is important." I informed him.

"I'll be the judge of how important this shit is nigga. I'll be right there. Better not be playing no games either motherfucker." Ace warned before hanging up.

Fifteen minutes passed as I walked up onto the bridge looking at the memorial that they started for my nigga Big 9. That shit would haunt me every fucking day.

One minute he was here then the next he was gone. He was offed for being a loyal ass motherfucker. Damn, I never thought we would be here.

"What the fuck do you want nigga and this better be fucking good to." Ace threatened.

When Ace looked out at the memorial, I wondered if he knew what really happened to Big 9. If he didn't, I was sure about to fill him in.

"Look I am here to warn you. This nigga HB is out for blood. I know right now you don't know if you can trust me or not but Snake was like my bro nigga. Never in a million years would I ever hurt y'all. I joined forces with HB only cause he threatened my family Ace. No one goods after my girl or my kids." I huffed.

"What the fuck is your point nigga? How and why the fuck did you ask me to come here?" I could tell that he was pissed off from the tone in his voice.

"Look HB is taking out anyone who stands in his way. Now that fool wants me to take Toni out." I confessed as he grabbed his piece and pointing it to my head.

"Give me one reason why I shouldn't take your sorry ass out. Huh. You want to kill Queenie's mom. Nigga you must be asking to die right where y'all dropped Big 9's body. Bitch I ain't dumb. I know why you brought me here. Guilt is eating your sorry ass up and to think my brother trusted you." Ace spat.

A part of me wanted to tell him to pull the trigger because I did betray my brothers by joining HB, but I had to think about my family. Shit, slanging was all I knew. Nothing else. I damn sure couldn't support my family off of no minimum wage job. Nigga had to do what he had to do.

"Look Ace, I came to tell you. I ain't looking for no reward or shit, just a warning. Your brother is my bro. I know that I fucked up but I am trying to help. Watch your back. He is out for war." I said as he placed the safety back on his piece and put it away.

I turned walking off. I felt defeated. It was so sad how that nigga didn't have trust in me. I wouldn't trust me either. I was rolling with HB who was a snake ass nigga that wanted to bring down everyone for his own personal gain.

That was some sad shit for sure...

Chapter Twelve

Toni

I guess my message got sent through the streets loud and clearly.

Don't fuck with me.

I wanted those niggas to know I was not the one to play with.

You play with fire you get burn; you play with Toni your ass get smoked. If you know what I mean. You come for me and mine. Nigga I come for you and yours.

I knew for a fact that HB wasn't too happy that I sent a couple of Slick Rick's niggas to shoot at him and his punk ass crew. I wasn't trying to kill anyone. It was just to send the messages that dead or alive Slick would always make sure me and mines were alright. Even if it meant a couple of niggas ended up in a body bag. It was just the way it was.

Noise echoed through the streets that HB wanted the motherfuckers responsible for Trigga's death. I couldn't lie. That shit tore me up inside when I heard that he had a baby on the way. Another black kid growing up without a dad. All he was going to do was join a crew and try to get the love that he lacked from his father cause he was murdered before he was born.

This shit made me sick to my stomach but a battle with TBone was the last thing that HB really wanted. I've done see that nigga at his worst and HB ain't no match for him.

TBone was known for cutting up niggas and delivering them to someone in your crew. He was heartless with no care the world for anyone.

I ain't worried about any of these punk ass niggas in HB's crew. Can't none of these niggas see me. Ain't none of them even qualified to take me out or even live to talk about it.

I may have had my problems in the past but protecting my daughter was a must. Slick taught me a long time ago that pussy ass niggas always sent someone else to do their dirty work. I wasn't worried about shit then because my focus was on Kera.

Damn, my baby girl had been through enough and the last thing I wanted was to allow anyone to try to hurt her when she was already at the lowest part of her life.

Doctors were continuously telling me that there was nothing that they could honestly do for her until she woke up. The chance of that happening was slim to none.

I refused to believe that this was it. *This can't be it.*

I sat on the bed running my hands through her soft but thick black hair as I heard footsteps walking up behind.

"Tell me that it's not true?" the voice asked.

It was TBone standing there with water filled eyes. Damn, the man I never thought I would have to face again was there.

Looking at TBone, the words wouldn't come out about how sorry I was. I took him away from his child and it still hurt me every day. I was a punk. I couldn't face Slick and tell him that I got wasted and fucked his main man, so I lied and said I didn't know who I was pregnant by.

I knew when Kera came out though, just who she belonged to and it made me not want her. I couldn't raise my daughter and look at Slick and not tell him the truth. Now look, I was losing them all.

I couldn't stand looking at myself knowing I was the one to cause my daughter so much pain. I hated myself every day for the pain that I caused Kera.

"I am so sorry Terrance. Yes. It's true. She is your daughter. I …. I can't begin to tell you how sorry I am." I apologized as he walked around the bed to the other side of Kera. He just looked at her. There were tubes all in her mouth and her eyes closed.

"Everything I ever wanted and you took it from me. Slick Rick was my bro he would have understood that we fucked up. It was you that chose to keep my daughter away from and now she is in this condition. This is fucking wrong. I could have stepped up Toni and been a man and took care of my mines like I do my sons but you didn't give me that opportunity." He fussed calmly.

He was right. I was so fucking selfish. No one's feelings mattered when I was getting high.

Only that I needed that fix and I didn't give a damn what anyone else had to say about it. Funny thing was, your thoughts and feeling always had a way of coming back to bite you in the ass every time.

"I know that sorry ain't going to fix shit but that's all I got. I didn't know what I wanted at that time Terrance. You were married and had a family. We fucked one time and I got pregnant. My biggest mistake was giving Kera to Harlem and not telling you. Now because of my choices my daughter is lying here fighting for her life. I hope Harlem rots in hell for doing this to my baby."

"Wait I know damn well you didn't allow that bitch to raise our daughter. What the fuck you mean? Harlem is the reason for this?" He questioned as Kera flat lined again.

My heart began pounding as the nurses and doctor came running in with the cart.

"I need you to go outside. Please." The nurse requested.

TBone grabbed my arm pulling me out the door. Tears poured down my face as they closed the door behind us. Just the thought of losing Kera was making me hate myself and my sister a hell of a lot more.

"What's going on?"

Ace came running down the hallway. His face worried.

"Toni what happened?" he asked barely getting the words to come out.

"She coded ..." TBone answered as Ace gave him the weirdest look.

"Nigga who the hell are you?" he asked harshly.

"You must be Black's son. You look just like that nigga. My name is TBone and I am Kera's pops. I heard about your brother Snake man, my condolences. Oh, and thanks for keeping an eye out for my daughter all these years." TBone blurted out.

"Are you the nigga that popped Trigga? Is this the nigga?" he said ass the doctors opened the door coming back out.

My chest pounded rapidly worried about what the hell they were about to tell me.

"We were able to resuscitate your daughter again, but it's not looking good right now ma'am. I really truly think it's time to let her go. To be honest ma'am her chance of recovering is very slim. I am sorry but the longer she stays in a coma the lower her chances of recovery are." The doctor said as my eyes filled with water.

TBone grabbed me, scooping me up in his arms for the first time ever and took me out of the room. My emotions took over as the tears poured from my eyes.

I placed my feelings to the side and focused on Kera. Just hearing that my baby would never recover was tearing me up inside. All I wanted to do was hold her one more time and tell her how I loved her. All the times of me being selfish had come down to this. Me missing out on the important things like my daughter...

Ace gave me and TBone a moment out in the hallway as he walked into the room to sit with Red. I think I saw a tear fall from his eye when the doctor said what he said. Ace had been there since day one. Losing his brother and now the possibility of losing Red was a lot for anyone to take in. As a mother the feeling was even worse.

The more I look at Red the more I just wanted to take my own life so she could live but I knew that wasn't how it worked. I would do anything just to have more time with her. I wish I could turn back the hand of time. I would do everything over. Be a better mother, a better wife and a better person.

I still felt bad about what happened before Slick Rick died. That man loved me beyond all my flaws. He took in my daughter after my sick ass brother in law raped here over and over again.

After that I felt the marriage was over. I went out and started back fucking with TBone. I mean Slick changed. He stayed out later and later. He would come home smelling like some bitch's cheap perfume and he started treating Kera different. I felt that a part of him knew that TBone was my baby's father.

Our last conversation still played over and over again in my head.

"Where the hell have you been Slick?" I asked as he walked into the house late again.

"Bitch, I've done told you about asking me motherfucking questions, but since you asking questions and shit who the fuck is Kera father? Huh? You gonna be a woman and tell me?" He asked boldly as I sat up on the bed.

"Look, Slick I told you before that I didn't know and keep your voice down before she hears you. Why don't you tell me whose cheap ass perfume that is that I smell on you? You want to talk about me and nigga while you fucking my sister? Bitch I ain't dumb I know her scent. What is her baby yours? Huh?" I questioned looking at him dead in the face.

My blood was boiling because I knew in my heart that he had been fucking my sister Harlem. That bitch thought that everything I had she can fuck. Damn, she had her own loser of a husband. Why the fuck would she fuck my man? Hell, he was just as nasty as she was.

"You know what bitch. I am not doing this shit tonight. I will be back later." Slick snapped.

I gave him the nastiest look that I could. I couldn't do this shit anymore. I was tired of sneaking around with TBone. I had just rather be with him anyways.

Suddenly the police busted into our home. I could have just shit my fucking panties. All I could think about was Kera asleep in the next room.

"Get on the ground now!" one office shouted. "Ma'am please move out of the way please!"

The cop that snatched up Slick yelled out, "Shawn Williams you are under arrest. Anything you say can and will be used against you in a court of law. If you don't have an attorney one will..."

The officer continued reading Slick his rights as they hauled his ass right on out the door. I looked as Kera stood in her doorway staring at the whole scene.

That was the last time I saw Slick Rick until his funeral. Before I had a chance to tell him anything he was killed. That shit still haunted me and now I was going through it again with my own flesh and blood. My baby...

Chapter Thirteen

HB

They say that: "Everyone suffers at least one bad betrayal in their lifetime. It's what unites us. The trick is not to let it destroy your trust in others when that happens. Don't let them take that from you." (unknown author)

Disloyal ass motherfuckers I couldn't fucking deal with. I tried to trust that nigga DMack and he fucked that up.

After True and Real told me the shit that he pulled I knew I had to follow that nigga to see what was really good. I sat in the car as DMack came out of his apartment building with a black ball cap on and his hoodie.

DMack must have really thought I was stupid. I knew what that fool looked like. We had been boys for years. I could spot his walk a mile away.

As he made his way, I followed him in my car. I couldn't say that it surprised me when I saw him meet up with that bitch Ace at the Harlem River. Some fools just didn't know how to learn about going against me.

DMack couldn't even off that bitch like I asked him to and now he was meeting with Ace behind my motherfucking back. Hell yeah he had to be dealt with now. He thought no one knew about that little family that he had, but I did. Snake told me about his girl and sons a while back. It was now time to hit that ass where it hurt.

I headed back to the block thinking about the way I was going to get DMack. I knew I should have never asked him to kill Toni. He had too much of a conscious to be a killer. He ain't have it in him.

See I offed that nigga Big 9 like it wasn't shit. Bro's or not. You with me or against me and if your against me then you had to be handled. It was a simple and plain as that.

I got to the house but it was still fucking with me so I decided to cut out and pay DMack a visit at his crib. Nigga dead ass fucked up by betraying me for that nigga Ace. On the real. Now I was about to show him.

I got to his apartment building and thought about my promise to hit DMack where it hurt, his family!

I stepped off the elevator onto his floor. Heading down the hallway, I watched as his shorty strolled out of the house carrying two suitcases. She set them beside the door before returning back inside. When she did, I grabbed the ski mask out of my pocket and quickly placed it over my head then crept into their apartment. Soon as I made it inside, I slammed the door. DMack's girl turned around in complete shock.

"Who the fuck are you? Get the hell out of my house now before I call the cops." She demanded.

Without thinking twice, I cocked back and rammed my fist into her face repeatedly. After about a dozen blows, I watched her as she fell onto the green colored carpet. I climbed on top of her chest and continued punching her.

Blood began gushing down from her nose and mouth but she was still trying to fight me off of her. When she finally gained up enough strength, she pushed me off of her and kicked me in my mouth.

"Hell na bitch," I thought to myself.

I began spitting the blood out of my mouth as I rose to my feet. Shaking the shit off I eyed DMack's bitch as she rolled over onto all fours trying to get up. I kicked her ass as hard as I could in her ribs repeatedly. Instantly she began gasping for air as she brought her knees up to her chest.

"Please... please stop. Take whatever you would want just please stop." She cried out in pain.

A part of me wanted to kick that bitch a couple of more times but I noticed she continued to hold onto her stomach and cry. Damn, I wanted to get my message across but not at the expense of an innocent child's life. I grabbed the phone dialing 911. When it started ringing I threw it down beside her before running out the door.

The whole way down the steps all I thought about was how she held onto her stomach. Damn, I may have killed a baby! Man that shit was really tearing me up inside.

I jumped into the car trying to pull myself together. As I started to pull off, my phone rung. It was that nigga True.

"What's good nigga?" I said picking up the phone.

"We got a problem. Need you to get here as fast as you can man!" He spat.

I could tell from True's tone that the shit was important. I sped off trying to get back to the block to see what could be up. When I hit the corner, I heard the sirens.

Damn, I really hope I didn't cause her to lose her baby. Shit, I wouldn't know what to do if I lost my son. Don't get me fucked up, DMack had that shit coming but his baby didn't.

While pulling up, all I could see were crowds of people looking. Seconds later, the ambulance parked right behind me.

"Damn, one of those junkies done fucking OD'd!" I thought to myself.

As I was getting out the car, True ran up to me covered in fucking blood.

"Yo nigga what the fuck happened? Wait whose the fuck blood is all over you?" I questioned looking at him to try and read him.

His faced had an expression that I had never seen before.

"Look nigga. A... A car came around blasting shots and um..." He started.

"Nigga spit the shit out. What the fucked happened?" I shouted before I heard Sophia scream out from a few feet away.

"Not my baby! He can't be dead! He's not gone! RJ get up! Baby boy please, get up!" Sophia cried out loudly.

I pushed passed everyone getting to the front of the line as quickly as I could. Soon as I did, the crowd split and I had a perfect view of my son's lifeless body lying on the cold cement. I fell down right beside him as I allowed the tears to pour down my face.

I couldn't believe that bitch Toni went after my kid. I underestimated her ass by a long shot.

I scooped RJ's little dead body up in my arms and cried, "These niggas killed my kid. These motherfuckers done really fucked up now. Ain't nobody safe. Not even Queenie.

"Sir, sir we need to take the body." The medic instructed.

I wiped my eyes and I kissed my son on his forehead. The hardest part was letting him go. That was my son man. They killed my fucking son man.

Real tapped me on the shoulder. I stood to my feet laying my baby's' body down on the stretcher. I kissed him once more then stepped back as they placed a sheet over him.

Before placing him in the van I walked over to Sophia as she still sat on the ground beside the bloody pool. Understandably the tears were still pouring down her face.

"Come on ma. Get up." I said grabbing her arm as she pulled away.

"Get the fuck away from me HB! This is your fucking fault right along with whoever killed my son! Now do something now! Right now before I do something!" She yelled before stomping off.

I wiped my face and stared down my crew. I wondered how the fuck they allowed that shit to go down. What the fuck had them so distracted?

Why weren't they on point with all that was happening? I didn't get the shit one bit.

"What the fuck happened nigga? How the fuck did my son get fucking popped." I spat trying to make sense of everything.

"Nigga scar rolled up blasting. I didn't know your shorty or seed was here until the car drove off. I don't know who would want to do that shit bruh but I can guarantee you that I popped a couple of rounds off on the passenger side. Those niggas ain't going to get away with this HB." Real promised.

"Fuck that shit kid. I know who did this shit. Now it's my turn to retaliate. First, kill that bitch Red. They took mine. I take theirs." I huffed.

"Are you sure bro?" True checked.

I pulled out my piece pointing it at his fucking head. How dare he question me at a time like that!

"Now nigga are you going to do this or do I have to splatter your brains all over this motherfucking building. Now kill that bitch or I'll kill you." I threatened as Real grabbed my arm.

I lowered my weapon sticking it back into my pants.

"Aight nigga damn, but cuz, don't you ever point no fucking piece at me again unless you're going to blast off. Aight nigga?" True shot back before walking off.

Folks might have thought shit was crazy before but now that they had killed my son it was war time. No one was safe in the game anymore.

I peeled myself away from everyone, trying to clear my head but yet I couldn't.

Is this my punishment for beating the shit out of that niggas DMack's old lady killing his seed?

I didn't give a fuck about anything after that shit. I didn't care about Brotherhood, loyalty or nothing. RJ was all I had left in the world and they took him from me.

They always said that you didn't know what you had until it was gone and damn if it wasn't true. My whole fucking world was shattered and to try to piece it back together wasn't even worth it.

I want revenge for my son. I am going to get revenge. Watch and see.

Chapter Fourteen

DMack

What the fuck? I thought to myself as I walked up to my apartment and the door was wide open. I pulled out my piece as I looked inside to Nicole lying on the ground.

You can't be fucking serious. This nigga came after my fucking family.

I ran into the house kneeling down beside my wifey. Blood continued pouring out her face. I could tell that she was in a whole lot of pain.

"Nikki, baby, hold on. Hold on baby." I pleaded.

Picking up my phone, I dialed emergency services. Funny thing was I could hear the sirens already. When I looked over at Nicole's cell, I saw that she had been on the line with 911. I didn't know if she called or if that nigga called the police after he did it. If he did, he must have felt guilty.

"Hold on baby please." I begged.

"The baby." she whispered.

"I haven't checked on them yet. Just hold on. The ambulance is coming. Please Nicole! I am so sorry baby about all this shit." I apologized.

She continued holding onto her stomach as blood dripped down from her mouth. I grabbed ahold of her hand and held it tightly until the ambulance finally arrived.

At the hospital I sat in the waiting room with my boys wondering what the fuck was going on. How the hell did I let this shit go this far.

Out of the blue, Nicole's mother Jackie ran into the waiting room. Her face was blood shot red. She rushed straight up to me and slapped the shit out of me. She was so damn lucky that it wasn't the time or place for that shit because my reflexes were about to knock that bitch the fuck out.

"This shit is all your fault. I told my daughter to stay away from motherfuckers like you. Now look. She is laying up in here. Where the hell is my child?" she hollered at the doctor.

"Doc, is she okay?" I asked standing there holding my youngest son in my arms.

"She suffered massive bruising and several broken ribs. We were able to stop the internal bleeding but she did lose the baby. Right now she is in a lot of pain and we are going to keep her here for a few days." he explained.

That information right there was enough to push a nigga over the edge. I held it together though...

When we got the green light for visitors, I allowed her mother to go into the room first because I knew that she wasn't feeling me. Meanwhile, I paced the waiting room until I saw Ace and Monika walk by.

"Yo Ace. Can I holla at you for a second? "I yelled out in his direction.

"I'll be right back." he told his old lady.

The look on his face warned me that he was leery. He didn't trust me one damn bit.

"Yo, listen I wanted to tell you about Big 9 but that nigga was tripping saying anyone that wanted to hold loyalty to Snake he was killing. That nigga Big 9 died because of his loyalty. Now because of mine, my old lady is laying in the hospital from a beating he gave her. Man, she lost my seed. I want this nigga yo. I want this nigga to pay for all the shit that he is doing to all of us. It's time to take this nigga out. Dead ass. Snake was my bro. His nigga took up for me more times than I can count." I ranted.

"Look, DMack I respect your loyalty to my brother but don't worry about HB and his punk ass crew. He will be dealt with. It's time to get out of the game and focus on your family." he said truthfully.

"Bro, I want this nigga man. He came after my motherfucking family kid. You know how we do it in the street. Dead ass I need you kid. Please Ace." I pleaded looking at him seriously.

"Alright listen, meet me at midnight. We will make this nigga pay for this shit." Ace promised.

"No doubt man." I said as I dapped my bro up.

Damn man losing Ant, Snake, Ty and almost my girl made me realize that my family meant more to me than street life. It was about time to leave that shit alone. Right after I made HB pay for the shit that he had done to me and my family.

I waited before I started walking into the room to see Nicole. Her mother took the boys to the house with her. The last thing I wanted was for my boys to see their mother that way.

When I closed the door behind me, I looked at the love of my life lying in a hospital bed in pain. I never thought that this life would lead to my wifey being hurt or my family being in danger.

"Come in babe." she said clearing her throat.

I eased on over to her and sat on the bed as she laid her head on my chest.

"Babe, I am so sorry. I never meant for this shit to happen to you. I'll take care of it though." I assured.

Sophia sat straight up in the bed. She sighed a little from the pain.

"DMack, I don't need you doing anything stupid. Stop trying to get revenge on everything. Is this what you want to teach our sons. Huh? To fucking get revenge. Baby sometimes you have to learn to walk away." she said.

"I almost lost you. We lost our baby. Nigga's need to learn. In the streets we don't play this shit. I swear if Snake was here this shit would have never went down." I fussed.

"Snake is dead. Do you want to be like him? Baby, I am not going nowhere and I don't wanna lose you behind no bullshit. Now promise me you won't go and get revenge. Please." she begged.

Just the thought of losing Nicole and my family had my head fucked all up. I knew that Nicole didn't want me to go after HB but he put his hands on my lady.

"Bae what are you thinking about?" Nicole questioned as she hit the side of her bed motioning for me to scoot up a bit.

I could tell that her mind was on me and making sure I didn't do something stupid to put me back in jail. As a young nigga I went to kiddie jail for about two seconds behind killing this nigga for almost killing my mother. I got locked up for eighteen months. That was the past and Nicole was my future.

I knew from the first time that I saw her that she was going to be mine. She was going to be my lover and my friend.

Back then I promised her the world and I was trying my best to keep my word, but not if it meant losing her or my sons in the process. That was something that I refused to do.

"I'm not thinking about nothing ma. I just want you to focus on getting well and let me focus on everything else." I suggested.

I wrapped my arm around her as she began to drift off to sleep. Right as she began to snore, a safe knock came to the door. It was that nigga Ace.

I softly lifted my shorty Sophia as I got up to go to the door to see what he wanted.

"What's good man?" I questioned in a low tone while looking back at Nicole to make sure that she was still sleeping

"Yo, nigga I heard that RJ was shot and killed today. Word is that HB and Sophia is searching revenge on that little niggas death. Shit is fucking real kid. You know the first person he is going to try to come after is Queenie and we can't let that shit happen. We need to take care of this nigga tonight." He said staring me down.

I didn't feel bad for HB. He killed my unborn child and someone killed his son. Who by the way we all thought was Snakes. Little nigga even looked like my nigga but that thot of the year Sophia claimed that the baby was HB's. Bitch was playing Snake and Queenie from the very beginning. I didn't feel bad for them at all.

What was done in the dark always came out in the light.

Suddenly, the intercom went off. "Code Red ICU! Code Red ICU!"

"Oh shit, that's where Red's at!" Ace spat. "Nigga stay here with your girl. Call you if I need you."

Ace took off running down the hallway. I shook my head and walked back into the room as Nicole eyes where opened. I knew that shit was going to happen. I just hoped and prayed that it wasn't Queenie again.

Fifteen minutes past and I finally received a text from Ace saying that it wasn't Queenie. It was another woman that lost her battle to cancer.

I exhaled as the nurse walked in to check Nicole vitals. I walked out the door while she did it.

"Damn"

Here came HB bringing his bold ass down the hallway coming towards me. That fool had truly lost his fucking mind bringing his sorry ass anywhere near us after what he had done to my shorty.

I think this nigga really wants to be placed on his ass right here and now. I don't give a fuck if we are in a hospital. Shit, this hospital ain't got security or cameras any damn way. I can really get away with killing this bitch.

"Well, well, well, if it aint the trader of the year DMack. I guess you see the message that I sent your trifling two timing ass huh?" He clowned.

I stood my ground and was ready for whatever that nigga tried to send my way.

"Nigga you got balls showing up here after what the fuck you did to my shorty. You're playing a dirty game HB and from what I heard, now you see how your dirt causes you to lose the ones you love. Huh? Like Snake would always say, 'God don't like ugly and I know he ain't t fond of you'. Since you killed my unborn child. Nigga you lucky I don't drop your ass right here and now." I threatened.

"You talking really hard right now motherfucker. What the fuck are you gonna do trader. I wonder what your shorty would say if she really knew what you do for a living. Next time you're given a task you do it."

"Nigga there will never be a next time. Now rise the fuck up out here before I do something I might regret." I promised as Ace walked up pointing his piece at the back of HB's head.

"Real niggas never sneak up by putting a gun to someone's head like a little bitch." HB rambled causing Ace to smirk.

"Nigga you don't know the half of what any real nigga does cause you ain't never been a real anything, except a real joke. Now rise the fuck up outta here or get a hot one to head. Either way is fine with me." Ace warned as he took the safety off his piece.

"This shit ain't over little Ace." HB promised before standing down.

"You are right man. Your time is coming. You can bet on that shit." Ace replied while putting his gun away.

Losing Snake had made Ace not tolerate shit from any one. If that nigga HB knew what was good for him he would vanish forever.

Chapter Fifteen

Ace

Looking at Red like that let me know what I needed to do. Shut the game down for good.

Folks had been in the game for way too long and all it had done was destroy families and our lives. Shit we done lost to many bro's in this game and I refused to lose anymore.

My brother Snake was lying six feet in the ground never coming back and those niggas still out there trying to do the same shit.

I remembered how Red used to tell me.

"The game can make you and it can destroy you and little bro it's destroying me. I got in it for all the wrong reason. I wanted to seek revenge for what happened to my family. But look what it has caused. It has caused me to be a monster. I don't want you like that you're my husband's little brother. Please don't be like me. Reggie wouldn't want this for you."

Red said that shit two weeks prior to her tragedy. That shit was eerie.

Red always wanted a fresh start but it was like she was never able to with that bitch Harlem and that punk ass nigga Roc on her back. Now no one knew what was going to happen.

As the clock struck midnight, I kissed Monika on the head as she slept in the chair beside Red. She looked comfortable so I didn't disturb her.

Red eyes were closed again. She could open and close them but that was all. Doctors were saying that she was in a vegetative state and might stay that way forever.

I went over to Red kissing her on the head before walking out the room. I took the stairs to the next level above Red to go get DMack from his shorty's room.

Somehow I was still trying to figure out if I could trust him. With everything that was going on it was hard to know who to trust in this game. Everyone was out for something, including him.

I stood at the door as he laid in the bed with Nicole. Damn, man it sucked seeing his wifey pay for choices that we continued to make. We should have all known that HB was no good. Now we had to deal with this bullshit until we took that ass out and tonight was going to be that night.

No more talking, no more bullshit. It's game over time. This nigga is going to pay for everything he did to me, my brother Snake, Red, Ty, Big 9; he'll for the whole motherfucker team. It's time to destroy this nigga once and for all.

I tapped at the window waking DMack up. He slowly moved his girl over and got out of the bed. He nodded his head letting me know he was ready. If we wanted to protect the ones we love we had to do it tonight!

We had a couple of cats from the block that respected my bro keep a watch out on HB to see where the fuck he was heading. Now that his son was gone and I put a gun to the back of his head I knew he was getting prepared for battle. It was one which only one person could win, that was me!

DMack grabbed his shoes as he started to the door. Nicole woke up and she looked at the both of us.

"Baby please be safe. Come back to me." she begged nearly in tears. He walked over to her placing a wet kiss on her lips.

"I will be back. I promise. I love you." He said as he turned heading to me.

I looked at him. I could tell he was ready but the thought of leaving his wife there all alone tore him up inside.

"Nigga are you ready?" I questioned making sure he was down with what we were about to do.

"Let's end this motherfucker bro." He said as I dapped him up.

We took the stairs down to the garage where I parked my car at. I could hear footsteps as we reached our floor. Before I could turn around, I felt a gun to the back of my head. Oh, that was a bitch ass move right there.

"I told this nigga to handle y'all but I guess he couldn't so now it's mine turn. Y'all sorry ass motherfuckers is the reason why my son is dead and now I think it time that you joined him." Sophia said aiming at us the barrel of that Glock 45. *Who the fuck do this bitch think that she is?*

One moment the bitch was at my house crying on my motherfucking shoulder now she wanted to have a motherfucking heater in my face.

"Bitch you got to be dumb as fuck to even think that you're going to pull that trigger and make it out of here alive. Now drop this gun before you piss me the fuck off." I warned as a gun fired.

"What the fuck?" I thought looking myself up and down then checking DMack.

Suddenly Sophia fell to the ground. Blood was pouring out from her head. I looked at DMack but his piece never came out of his shoe.

"*Who the fuck shot this bitch*" I wondered until I saw a car pulled up. It was Black.

"Y'all niggas waiting on a fucking invitation or something? Get the fuck in the car." He ordered.

With no questions, we both got into the car. "How the fuck does this nigga always know when I am going to do something?"

I have to do something that he has never done before and that was to protect me and my family. Niggas in the hood kept talking about how good my pops was but that nigga wasn't shit. He protected the hood better than he ever protected me or Snake. Now he wanted to act like a dad; now that my brother was gone. It was a little too late for that shit, on the real.

Sometimes when I looked at my dad I got sick to my fucking stomach. Just knowing that this man never wanted me. He just got my mom pregnant and bounced. Not like she was any better when she left me with my GMom when I was three days old. My GMom raised me.

I knew that she was looking down from heaven pissed about all the bad choices that I had made. She always used to tell me, "Baby, God has your back when no one has it. Remember that".

After she was murdered I quickly learned that no one had your back. You had to fight on your own and now with Monika in my life I had to fight for her too.

We pulled out the parking garage as I waited for Black to say something smart. Just anything...

"I know right now Ace your hurting and you feel like this is the only way to handle it but son I am telling you it's not." Black said as I looked at him. My face instantly frowned up with disgust.

"Nigga you don't know shit. You can't begin to imagine the shit that I am feeling. Stop sitting here putting on this bullshit role of daddy alright nigga. Cause it's a little too late for that shit." I blurted out with no regards to his feelings.

"You know what little nigga, I done let you slide with all you Slick ass remarks that you keep coming at me with cause I know you was and still is trying to figure out how to handle your brother's death, but I am warning your ass right now. You keep coming for me and I am going to kick your ass. I made my share of mistakes but nigga I am still your pops." He stated firmly.

"Barely, shit, you know what nigga pull the fuck over. We can do this shit ourselves." I huffed as he flicked on his blinker pulling over the car getting out. When he walked over to my side, in my head I was wondering what the fuck he was doing.

I found out real quick when Black opened the door and heaved me out. Then, the nigga had the nerve to throw me up against the car.

"Let me make one motherfucking thing clear to you nigga. I don't tolerate shit from no little shit talking hustler and I ain't gonna tolerate that shit from my own son. You think you're the only motherfucking person hurting? Well you're not Ace. Yeah I fucked up man. I should've been a man and helped your grandmother out when she was raising you but I was nothing but a fucking boy myself. I wasn't ready to be no damn man. I fucked up you and Reggie's life. You think I don't beat myself up about that shit every damn day? Well I do. I fucked up and there ain't no way I can take back all that time. I lost one son. I don't want to lose you too Ace. I am fucking sorry son." He apologized.

For the first time that shit felt real. I knew Black meant everything he was saying.

I threw my arms around my pops. Losing my brother made me realize how much I needed my pops. No matter what shit that we went through, He was still my dad. Plus, with all the shit that was going on with Red I needed him in my corner.

After a few moments I released my pops and we got back into the car. I looked back at

DMack and he smiled a little. Damn, I think that was the first time that I ever seen that nigga smile.

"Where is this nigga at?" My pops questioned.

I picked up my phone and dialed up my spy.

"Yo, nigga where y'all at?" I inquired.

"Roc's old spot."

"Alright nigga. You better not try no Slick shit True." I warned.

"No worries, I got you nigga." He guaranteed as I hung up.

I knew that DMack was stuck on stupid. He thought he was the only person letting me know what the fuck is going on. Hell na. Me and my nigga True went way back. He may be Sophia's cousin and all but GMom used to babysit that nigga when we was little and shit. He spent more time at my crib then his own. Shit when GMom died that nigga took as hard as I did. Hell the whole block did.

GMom was the hoods mom. She fed people when they were hungry and everything. She was a true saint.

We wound up falling out after GMom's death but when I came at him not that long ago it was like we were never beefing. When shit jumped off with HB, True hit me up from the very beginning and kept me in the loop about everything.

Flashback...True and Ace

I decided to go visit my brother's body the day before his service. That shit was truly tearing me up but I knew that it was something that I had to do.

As I marched up the street I could feel the presence of someone behind me.

"Don't turn away empty out your pockets Ace."

The only bitch ass person to call me that was that nigga True. He never let me live that shit done after my ex-girlfriend Paula started calling me that. She thought it was cute and shit.

I turned around looking this nigga in the eyes. "I knew it was only your bitch ass that would call me some shit like that. What the fuck are you doing here bro?" I asked dapping my bro up.

"My cousin Sophia called me to work with this nigga HB and shit but you know how I am about working with new people and shit. Fool already acting stupid and shit. Popped a nigga for

*being loyal. Oh sorry about your brother kid." He
said.*

*"Don't trust that nigga bro. He's a fucking
Snake and he's gonna end up ordering you take me
out. He don't like me and he didn't like my brother."*

*"Bro don't even worry about that shit. I got
you kid. Plus, we grew up together. GMom treated
me just like I was hers. Nigga you ain't got to worry
about shit. That nigga ain't gonna touch you bro.
Where was you headed nigga?" he said.*

*"I was going up to the funeral home to see
my bro before the funeral and shit. Trying to roll
with me." I offered.*

*"Yeah nigga. I know this shit is hard. No one
deserves to deal with this alone. Dead Ass." He
replied as we headed down the street to the funeral
home.*

*My heart raced as we approached the place
that was holding my brothers body. I never thought
that I would have to do this.*

*After taking a deep sigh, we walked up to
the door of the chapel. A part of me didn't have the*

strength to go in but then a part of me knew that I didn't have any other choice.

I pulled myself together and entered the small building. The chaplain greeted us and led us to where my brother's body laid resting in peace.

Slow music played in the background and made my emotions take over. I tried to stay strong.

"Damn"

True sat down in the back as I walked up to my brother's casket. Tears cascaded down my face as I continued to look at Snake lying in something that I never thought he would be in. I mean I knew one day but not this soon.

"Why you man? We had more work to do big bro, but don't you worry. I'm going to shut this game down. I promise you that.' I spat as I walked out the door.

"Ace...Ace..." DMack yelled bringing me back.

"What nigga??" I snapped.

"True? What the fuck is that shit all about?" He said as I looked at my pops.

"Nigga, I hope you didn't think you was the only nigga playing both sides. My GMom helped raised that nigga True. I knew that nigga since we were in diapers. You feel me. This nigga is like family but forget all that I hope you're ready nigga we need to end this shit here and now." I said hoping that he was up for the shit we were about to do.

I didn't need him to bitch up later. We needed to handle HB once and for all.

Chapter Sixteen

Toni

I once heard a quote that says: 'I don't know how my body stays together when my soul is completely broken.' (Sandra Heavenbeans book Angel).

I waited as the doctor tried to run more tests on Kera to see if there was any change in her condition or any signs of life left at all. TBone decided to come back up today with his sons so that they could meet their sister. How things looked that might have been the last time they would get to see my baby girl alive.

She was dying and no matter how hard I wanted her to get better it was just not turning out that way. Never thought that I would be in a situation in which I would have to bury my own daughter.

"Damn, I can't believe it!"

We sat in the waiting room as Monika grabbed ahold of my arm holding on tight. I knew the last time the doctor had to bring her back he said her chances of recovering was slim to none.

"Are you okay T?" TBone checked as he came and sat down beside me.

I kept fighting back my emotions when they wanted to completely take over me. All of my hoping, wishing and praying to God but nothing seemed to work. God ain't listening to a woman that had done so much wrong.

TBone looked at me and paused for a response as the doctor entered the room. My heart began racing out of my chest hoping that maybe we could get some good news this time.

"We have run all the possible tests on your daughter and I am sorry to say that her condition has only worsened. I am so sorry. There is nothing else we can possibly do for her now." The doctor revealed truthfully.

My worst thoughts had arrived. I now had to make the decision to either let my daughter go or allow her to suffer more than what she was suffering already. *What the hell do I do?*

The doctor walked off leaving a burning pain in my chest. There was confusion, angry, hurt and pain. It was just about every emotion I could possibly feel.

"I am so sorry Toni." Monika whispered.

I knew that she was sincere, but the last thing I wanted to hear from anyone was some damn... I'm Sorry! Sorry wasn't going to make my decision any easier. Sorry wasn't going to wake my daughter up. Sorry wasn't going to do shit so I didn't want to hear the shit!

I made my way down the hallway as I stopped in front of the Chapel. Maybe God is sending me a message. I entered and fell to my knees.

"Is this what you want? I'm bowing down to you! I'm begging you! Please spare my daughter's life! Please Lord, please!" I screamed.

Suddenly a hand touched me. It was on my shoulder and I didn't move.

"T, come on ma. Get up. This is not your fault alright. This is not your fault. I know right now nothing no one will say can make you feel better.

What do you want to do, huh? Talk to me ma. What do you want to do about our daughter's condition. It's a hard decision but we got to make this one together." TBone said as I sat down.

For the first time in my life I got to make a decision on what was best for Kera and I was scared. I didn't know what to do but I was thankful to have her father there to help me do it.

I continued to sit with TBone wondering what the hell we were going to do. All of Kera's life I made all the wrong decisions. Who to raise her? Do I tell her that I am her mother? Do I tell her the truth of why I couldn't or didn't want to raise? Do I tell her the truth about her father. Just everything. Now I had a chance to make the right decision. I just wasn't sure what it was.

After sitting in the Chapel for fifteen minutes, we headed back to our daughter's room. I walked up to the door as her brother stood in the room watching her, talking to her, protecting her. Tears pouring down their faces. Seeing them cry without even knowing Kera made emotions that I once tried to bury rise right back up again.

"Kera, I know that it took a long time for us to meet you, but here we are sis. It's crazy that you are in this position though, but don't worry about shit. Your name is gonna rain down on all the niggas that had something to do with this shit. Bet that Sis. These nigga don't know your big brothers, but they will." TBone's son TJ said as he kissed Kera on her head before heading out the door.

I stood stunned as I viewed the intimate moment between Kera and her brothers. It hurt me to think that it was the only interaction that they were going to have.

I continued to watch as TBone walked beside me. He didn't want to leave my side.

His son's finished up and stormed out of Kera's room and down the hallway pissed off. That was a feeling I knew all too well.

Finally, we were in the room alone with our baby girl. I slowly sat down on the bed rubbing my hands through my angel's hair. I knew that it was time to let her go. As hard as it was to say, I needed to let my daughter finally rest in peace.

"Kera, baby if you are in there, I need you to know a few things. First off baby girl I love you and I am extremely sorry that I didn't tell you the truth about me. I was so afraid of losing the only person that showed me what it meant to love someone. Everything that happened to you was definitely my fault and I know that now. I was young and stupid and was too afraid to fuck up your life. Even through it ended up that way anyways. Damn, I don't know what I am doing Kera. I messed up so bad baby I want you to know that I am sorry I wasn't there for you when your uncle used to rape you, I wasn't there when you thought Snake was dead or when you lost your baby and I wasn't there when Harlem shot you but baby I am here now to make the hardest choice of my life. The doctors are saying that there is nothing else that they could do for you. I know that you are tired baby and want to be with your family. I know it's time baby girl. I am not going to let you suffer anymore. Know that I love you Kera. God is going to be blessed to have an angel like you." I said kissing her on the head.

"This is what she wants." I told TBone as he came by me and grabbed ahold of my hands.

"It's time. I need to call everyone so they can come and say their last goodbyes." I said before retrieving my phone.

Needing some air, I left TBone sitting down on the bed next to Kera. I had to go outside and talk.

Ace ain't going to take this shit too well, but it's time. She is already gone. It's just her body that we are trying to keep alive.

As the phone rung my heart pounded fast because I couldn't believe the words that were about to come out of my mouth.

"Yo Toni, is everything alright? Is Queenie good? What's going on?" Ace questioned in a panic.

"I need you all to come back to the hospital. The doctor said that there is nothing else that he can do for Kera. So, I am about to have him pull the plug so she can finally be at peace and I want all of y'all here."

All of a sudden the phone went silent. I didn't know what the hell was going on in Ace's head but I knew it couldn't have been good.

"We are on the way." He sniffled before hanging up.

God give me the strength to get through this.

Chapter Seventeen

Ace

My urge to get HB was at an all-time high. I wanted that motherfucker to pay for all the shit that he had done to everyone. The more I thought about it the madder I got.

It's time to teach this nigga a fucking lesson. I'm tired of this nigga and his fucking mouth.

Black pulled up to the spot where HB was at. True had called me and gave me the heads up.

Getting that call from Toni made it harder for me to concentrate. All I could think about was that they were about to take my sis off of life support.

Those words echoed through my head like a broken record on repeat. *Damn, man this is some bullshit man* dead ass.

A major part of me wanted to get out of the car and deal with HB, but I refused to miss a moment to say good bye to Red. You never knew if you would get a second chance...

"Yo, nigga you good?" DMack checked.

I nodded my head affirmatively and filled them in on what Toni told me.

"Yo pops we need to get back to the hospital. They are about to pull the plug on Red. Docs are saying there's nothing else they can do. We will get this fuck boy later. Right now I need to be there for Toni."

I glanced back at DMack. His face had a surprised looked on it. It was like he couldn't believe what I was saying.

"Let's go then," Black replied jingling his keys.

We arrived at the hospital within a few minutes. Before the car could stop I jumped out running into the hospital all the way to Red's room. Monika greeted me with a warm hug.

I knew that pulling the plug on her daughter was one of the hardest decisions that Toni had to make. I didn't blame her though. Queenie has been suffering for months and the last thing I would want was to see her suffer any longer.

My phone rung and it was that nigga True. I walked away a little to answer.

"Hello? Yo, nigga what the fuck is going on?" I asked quietly.

"Well, well, well if it ain't Ace. I see now who the fuck this niggas been betraying my trust for. Your bitch ass. Once I get done with this bitch I am coming for you. This shit ends now nigga. It's all your fault that this nigga had to end up like Big 9, Snake and that bitch Red." HB stated harshly.

"Nigga I am going to fucking kill you! Let anything happen to True and your done."

When I stopped speaking, I heard a gun go off.

"His blood is on your hands now bitch! I am coming for you next." HB hung up without another word.

"Fuck!" I yelled punching a hole in the wall.

That nigga done killed the only fucking brother I had left. I had to destroy this bitch ass nigga once and for all.

The doctor walked down the hallway as I joined back up with Monika. My heart began to pound rapidly as we started piling into the room surrounding Red. I looked back as TBone stood beside two young niggas that looked to be a couple years older than Queenie.

In my mind I wondered who the fuck those nigga were but I knew now wasn't the time to ask any questions.

I took a hold of Toni's arm as the doctor began turning off the machines. Within minutes the machine that monitored Red's heart flatlined. The doctors waited a few minutes before calling it. Just like that she was gone.

"Time of death 4:30pm. Come on everyone. Let's give the family a minute." The doctor suggested as they turned off the rest of the machines before leaving out of the room.

Tears ran down Toni's face as she hugged Red. Man, I am telling you seeing my sis like that was fucking tearing me up.

I looked at DMack as he nodded his head. Now it was time to go get this nigga for Snake, Big 9 and Red.

We headed out the door and Monika ran behind me.

"Ace where are you going? Baby please don't do this. Ace I'm pregnant." Monika revealed stopping me dead in my tracks.

"What?"

"I have been trying to tell you for a while but it never seemed to be the right time..." she started.

"What did you say Monika?" I yelled.

"You're about to be a father and don't ever yell at me again. Whatever you're thinking about doing Ace it ain't worth it. He ain't worth it babe. Think about your family cause that's what we have now a family." Monika said as she started to walk away.

I grabbed her arm gently pulling her to me softly kissing her lips. I couldn't have been happier in a moment of sadness and confusion.

"Listen baby, nothing and no one will ever come before you and my child but right now I got something that I need to do. I promise you, I will be back. Stay here with Toni." I told her. "Monika, I love you."

Losing Red and finding out that my girl was pregnant, damn. I knew I had to end HB before he tried to come for my family.

My pops sat in the car as we jumped in. Without saying a word my pops pulled off. My feelings were all over the place.

GMom used to always say: "Ace, baby God doesn't make no mistakes. When bad things happen. A good thing happens as well. You never know what blessing God has for you baby but whatever it is you gotta be ready to receive it.

Now GMom wasn't always going to be there but I wanted to remember this: "Revenge doesn't ease the pain. It just makes it a hell of a lot worse."

She said that shit right before she was gunned down like an animal by some stupid ass little nigga that I was still hoping to find.

We pulled back up to the last place I knew HB was at. It looked a hell of a lot emptier now. Good, less witnesses.

I stepped out the car as I saw True laying on the ground. I ran over to him as his eyes popped open. I pushed down on the gunshot wound on his chest trying to stop the bleeding.

DMack got out the car putting his hands on top of mine. I moved my hands standing to my feet only to turn around to HB pointing a gun in my face.

Blood from my homeboy True dropped down my fingers onto the cold cement. Bitch ass niggas loved sneaking up on folks.

"I heard you was looking for me nigga. Well here I am. Now give me one good ass reason why I shouldn't blow your fucking head off. You know what? Maybe I should blow your head off, your pops, that nigga DMack, your girl and that bitch Red's head off. Yeah, that's what I'll do. You've been talking a little too much shit Ace. Now that you don't have your brother or Red here to protect you, you want to act hard but nigga you're softer than my son's ass. Yeah the same son y'all niggas took from me and now it's my turn to take something back in return." he warned before I cocked back and swung, knocking him down to the ground

His gun flew out of his hand landing beside me. I picked it up and aimed it at him. When I did, the nigga with him pulled out his piece and drew down on me.

"What are you going to do now little bitch? Real tell this nigga who the fuck you are." HB demanded as I pointed my piece at that fool.

"I am the nigga that killed your sweet ol' GMom. I wanted to just rob the bitch but she wanted to get all holy and shit so I popped her ass." He laughed casually.

"How does it feel to finally get to meet the nigga that popped old granny?" HB clowned as the both continued to laugh.

This sorry ass piece of shit killed my grandmother.

He continued to laugh until I pulled the trigger. The bullet pierced right in between his eyes shutting his mouth forever.

There was blood splatter all over the place while I watched his body fall back and hit the ground.

I walked over to HB and kicked him in the face as he tried to stand to his feet. I dropped the gun as I climbed over him punching his ass repeatedly in the face.

Nigga think that I give a fuck right now cause I don't.

We can hear the sirens as my pops tried pulling me off that nigga but I continued to swinging on him. I was uncontrollably busting him in his mouth.

"Yo, nigga we need to go right fucking now." DMack warned pulling me off of HB as I keep kicking at his sorry ass.

"Come on son. This nigga ain't worth it. Come on." He urged as HB slowly picked his gun up off of the floor.

"Yeah little bitch you better listen to your pops. Before I have to do something that I might regret later." He threatened.

Nigga still wanted to run his fucking mouth like he was crazy. I wasn't playing with that nigga. Man, on the real.

"You want to repeat that shit again nigga?" I asked.

HB pointed the gun at my face as the police pulled up. Their lights were flashing but that didn't make him lower his weapon.

Instead of coming to my aide, one cop ran over to True who was fighting to stay alive.

"Drop your gun Sir! We are not going to ask you again! Don't do it Sir! Don't shoot!" The police yelled as HB continued holding the gun aimed at my head.

"Go ahead nigga pull that trigger cause you're going to pay for everything fucking you did to my family. You aint shit HB but a snake ass nigga trying to show everyone how tough you're not. I can see right past your fake ass bullshit and so did my brother. That's why you was hoping he died. Your bitch ass should have pulled the trigger. Now who's the bitch? Oh, yeah, you are." I clowned.

"Fuck you ace! Nigga you think you knew your brother better than I did? Where the fuck were you or your pops at when that nigga needed you? Nowhere to be found, so save that shit for someone else. That nigga Snake wasn't all that! That nigga was a bitch. He killed Ant thinking that nigga was on ROC's side and it was me the whole time! Yeah, I played both sides and fucked his bitch in the process. Your brother wasn't shit!" he said taking the safety off the gun.

"Sir drop your weapon! We are not going to ask you again! Drop your weapon now!" the officer screamed again.

HB looked at me and tapped the trigger.

"No!"

The officers began firing back repeatedly knocking HB onto his ass. They moved in checking to see if he was alive and he wasn't. I guess he wanted to die like OG or something but that shit ain't happened. He was still a fake ass fool.

I felt a sharp pain as I felt the warmest of something drip down my arm.

"Oh shit Ace you're shot." My pops gasped as I fell to the ground.

Hours Later...

I woke up after what seemed like a long bad nightmare. I still couldn't believe that HB shot me man.

I opened my eyes as she sat on the bed beside me. *'This can't be real. Did I die? What the hell is going on right now?'* I continued to ask myself as I looked into Red's face.

"Hi Ace, why are you standing there looking like you seen a ghost or something?" She questioned.

"Did I die? Please tell me that I died?" I panicked. Red just sat there and giggled a little.

"No Ace you didn't die. I know right now everything is not making sense to you but I need you to stop blaming yourself for what happened to me and Reggie. It's not your fault. I was tired Ace. I fought all my life. I was so angry my whole life for the things that happened to me, my daughter,

Snake and the whole nine yards. Now I am at peace and you should be too. We just want you to do better and be better Ace. You have an opportunity to do anything that you want to, starting with your baby. Give your child something more to look up to. Live your life Ace don't let the streets live it for you. Learn how to forgive Ace. Black wasn't perfect but he is your father and you're going to need him like he is going to need you. Talking about forgiveness tell my mom I love her and forgive her. Tell her to stop blaming herself. It's not her fault either. I love you both. Live your life Ace. Now wake up!" Red said as I opened my eyes.

"Red!" I screamed as Monika sat up in the chair.

I looked to the right of me to see my whole world. Words couldn't begin to express how much that woman had changed my life. She made me want to be a better man and a father to our unborn child. Even though the pieces to the puzzle of my life was all fucked up, I knew that with Monika by my side all the pieces would find their way back to their own place. I truly didn't know what would do without her. Even though it was just a dream, everything that Red told me was true.

Forgiveness wasn't one of my strong points.

"Baby are you okay?" Monika asked as my nigga DMack walked into the door.

I wondered if that nigga True made it or not. Shit, the last thing I needed was to lose anyone else.

I felt super bad for Toni. She just got her daughter back only to lose her again. She had been trying to hold it together but I could tell that it was tearing her up inside. To know that she would never get to hold Red again, talk to her again or nothing, the shit wasn't fair man.

That nigga HB destroyed the fucking hood. Now these niggas wasn't ever going to be able to trust one another. They were going to hear the story and start doubting their own niggas loyalty.

The game was through for right now. Police wasn't playing that shit anymore. All the deaths we had in the last year, the police was going to lock all the wannabe's up.

"Yo, nigga how are you feeling?" DMack said dapping me up as the sharp pain stung from the bullet hole in my fucking arm.

"You know nigga shit is the same. Yo, how's True?" I asked as DMack held his head down.

"They tried Ace. He died on the surgery table. I am really sorry my nigga." He said as I held back my tears.

I guess it was a good thing that the police took that sorry piece of shit out instead of me.

It wasn't long before Toni showed up to check on me. Her eyes were swollen and red from crying all night. The fact of knowing that Red was really gone left a hurt spot in all of our hearts.

We never thought that we would have to deal with the pain again so soon. I truly thought that she was going to pull through.

"DMack, let's give them a minute." Monika suggested as she kissed me on the lips before heading out the door.

I didn't know what words to say to make her feel better. Shit, honestly I didn't think there were any words that could be said.

"Hi, T how are you holding up?" I asked sitting up in the bed.

"I don't know Ace. Nothing feels the same anymore you know. I walked to the room where she was at. Hoping that she would be there laying in that bed but she's not. She's not! I don't know what the hell I am going to do without her Ace. The funeral home already called asking me about her burial services. I don't know if I can do this alone Ace." she cried.

"Yo, T you ain't alone. I am right here. So are Monika and DMack. No matter what the situation is, know that we are here for you. We will help you get through this." I promised.

Chapter Eighteen

Toni

Losing my daughter had left a hard pain in my heart that I was not sure that anything or anyone could fix it. Seeing her taking her last breath tore me up inside. I never thought that Kera would die before me. Now I had to deal with the feeling and the shit was fucked up.

HB really destroyed my fucking life but I couldn't blame him. I did it to my fucking self.

Leaving Kera all these year ago and now seeing that it was too late to be a mother to my own child because she was gone was mind blowing. Now I had to deal with the shit for the rest of my life.

Shortly after leaving Ace I decided to go see TBone to see how he was holding up. I knew right now the last thing that he wanted was to hear how sorry I was. Shit I took him away from his daughter when we could have been a family.

I walked up to his apartment building as he sat down on the steps drinking a forty while smoking a fat ass blunt.

"T, what the hell are you doing here? How are you holding up?" TBone said as I sat down beside him.

"Not good at all TBone. I am trying to cope with it but it's hard as hell. Losing Kera has been the hardest thing to deal with right now. Terrance, I don't know how many times I can say sorry for what the hell I've done. I should have never kept you from your daughter and now she is gone and there's nothing that I could do about it. Nothing." I said as tears streamed down my face.

"Sorry can't fix this shit T. Damn, you know how bad I wanted a daughter. You knew that I never had parents so I wanted to be the type of father my father wasn't to me. You took that away from me. You know how I am with my boys but you decided to kept the only daughter I ever had away. Instead you just gave her to your stupid ass jealous sister as if she was a fucking gift that you can claim later when you were ready to fucking grow up. You knew I loved you. You knew I would have given Kera and you the world but instead you wanted to be a selfish bitch. Now look, my child is dead due to your sister's bullshit. I won't ever get to spend a fucking ounce of time with her. To explain to her why I wasn't there. Nothing. You think your fucking apology is supposed to mean something to me. It don't mean shit. Now if you don't fucking mind I would like to at least mourn my daughter's death in fucking peace." TBone snapped before taking a sip of his half gone forty.

"I am sorry TBone. I really need you to know that. I am going to the funeral home to make the plans for our daughter's funeral." I said as he looked at me still sipping on his forty.

My chest fluttered as I approached the funeral home. I really wished that I didn't have to lay my child to rest but I owed Kera so much for never being there for her the way that a mother was supposed.

I stood in front trying to get the courage to go inside. It took a minute.

"Toni, hey what are you doing here?" Miguel asked.

Looking into his eyes, I almost didn't notice that he held a beautiful little girls hand. Oh shit! I don't think that he knows that Kera is dead, but damn that little girl looked so familiar.

"Miguel, I have something that I have to tell you... UM... Kera's gone."

"But I thought... NO Toni! She can't be... she was fighting. She can't be." He cried.

"Whose Kera daddy?" the little girl questioned innocently.

"Baby I need you to go and stand by the stairs for me, please so I can talk to Mrs. Toni."

Miguel and I both watched as the little ran over to the stairs. I continued to look at her as I waited for Miguel to explain.

"Who's child is that Miguel? That little girl looks so familiar. Who's her mother?" I asked as we both continued to look at the little girl.

"She's mine and Kera's." He said as i was totally taken by that.

"Excuse me. You're telling me that this little girl is my granddaughter. How old is she? Miguel how old is she?"

"Nine. She will be ten next week. How do I tell my child her mother is gone?" he asked as I was still puzzled by the fact that the little girl was my daughter's child. I never knew... Wait, that meant that she was pregnant when she was living with me. How did I not know that my child was pregnant?

"Look... I have a lot of questions but, first what's her name?" I inquired curiously.

"Kayla. She always loved the name but she told me that you always told her if you ever had a daughter that you would've named her Kayla. When she looked at Kay she thought about you. That's why my mom and I raised Kay. Then, when she got pregnant by Roc and Snake she wanted to be a part of Kay's life and I said no. Now look it's too late. Come on Kay. Now I got to live with this for the rest of my life." Miguel said grabbing Kayla's arm before walking off.

Kera would never be able to see her daughter grow up. It was sad to see how our choices affected the ones that we loved even if it was not our intentions to do it.

****

The day had finally come for Kera's funeral. I hadn't seen or heard from TBone nor Miguel since our last talk. I knew that there was no amount of words to make things right.

I had heard that Ace was released from the hospital and planned to be there. It was at the church that she attended as a child. She used to say that it was her home away from home.

I sat in the limo finishing up the speech that I wanted to say to my daughter for the last time. I needed to say it before she was placed in the ground.

A knock came to the window as the door opened. It was TBone. Damn, he was looking really good in this suit. Made me think about the good times we used to have.

"What's up T? Look I am sorry about the other day. This shit has been really rough on me and shit. You know. I never imagined burying my kids before they buried me. I stopped by the funeral home after you left and paid for everything and even had them put Kera on a dress that you wore a long time ago. I had it fixed up to fit my princess." He informed me proudly.

"What dress?" I asked.

"The light blue dress that you wore when I took you out to dinner and proposed to you. You was all pregnant and shit. I knew then like I still know now that we are meant to be ma. I never stopped loving you Toni." TBone confessed as he leaned in trying to kiss me on the lips. I was nervous so I slid back.

"Look I don't want to get into this right now. Let's bury our daughter first before talking about this." I suggested.

I could tell that his feelings were hurt. That truly wasn't my intent.

"You're right. Damn, I wish Kera would've gave us a grandchild first." He sighed opening the door looking into Kayla's face. I could tell by the way he looked he knew that she was Kera's daughter. He grabbed my hand helping me out the car as Kayla ran into my arms.

"I am so sorry grandma." she apologized as I wrapped my arms around her holding her tightly. I never thought I would ever hear those words but hearing them let me know that everything was going to be okay.

I looked into Kayla's eyes and all I could see was my beautiful angel Kera. She would be happy to see the beautiful little girl her daughter had become.

DMack and Ace walked up placing their hands on my shoulder letting me know it was time. It was time to deal with a tough day.

I don't know if I will ever be ready for this. God please give me the strength to make it through.

I grabbed my granddaughter's hand as we headed into the church. As we entered, so did the local gangster and hustlers.

Kera was really loved and respected by everyone in the hood. That truly touched me to the core.

Music played softly in the background as we walked up to the Prim Rose Casket with my baby lying inside. She was indeed wearing my beautiful blue wrap dress that I wore the night her father asked me to be his wife. I loved how TBone made it to where it fit her so beautifully. Her makeup was lightly applied to fit the princess that she was.

I tried to hold back the tears but they rained down my face. I never thought that it would be this way, but looking down at her sleeping peacefully, I knew that the game was over.

OVER FOR GOOD!!!

From Author Destiny Henry

Every day in the world someone is dying due to gun violence. It's time that we take a stand and get communities back involved to stop the violence. Too many people, especially young kids are growing up without mothers and fathers due to gun violence. I recently lost a cousin and my niece was shot for being at a party when people just pulled out guns and started firing. Then, all the family is left to mourn the loss of someone they love. Let's drop the guns. Let's take a stand against gun violence. "Enough is Enough"

Thank you.

Rest in heaven Deon Geathers and all the people around the word that lost their lives due to gun violence.

CPSIA information can be obtained
at www.ICGtesting.com
Printed in the USA
LVHW041515200519
618483LV00014B/1147/P